SPOKEN FOR

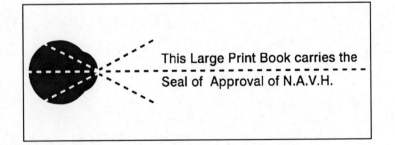

This Large Print Book carries the
Seal of Approval of N.A.V.H.

SPOKEN FOR

EMBRACING WHO YOU ARE
AND WHOSE YOU ARE

ROBIN JONES GUNN
AND ALYSSA JOY BETHKE

CHRISTIAN LARGE PRINT
A part of Gale, Cengage Learning

GALE
CENGAGE Learning®

Farmington Hills, Mich • San Francisco • New York • Waterville, Maine
Meriden, Conn • Mason, Ohio • Chicago

LIBRARY OF CONGRESS CATALOGING-IN-PUBLICATION DATA

Gunn, Robin Jones, 1955–
    Spoken for : embracing who you are and whose you are / by Robin Jones Gunn and Alyssa Joy Bethke. — Large Print edition.
        pages cm. — (Christian Large Print originals)
    Includes bibliographical references.
    ISBN 978-1-59415-502-4 (softcover) — ISBN 1-59415-502-X (softcover)
    1. Identity (Psychology)—Religious aspects—Christianity. 2. God (Christianity)—Love. 3. Gunn, Robin Jones, 1955– 4. Bethke, Alyssa Joy. 5. Large type books. I. Title.
BV4509.5.G83 2014
248.4—dc23   2014008065

Published in 2014 by arrangement with Multnomah Books, an imprint of the Crown Publishing Group, a division of Random House LLC

Printed in the United States of America
2 3 4 5 6   18 17 16 15 14

PERMISSIONS

From Robin:
To all my nieces: Amanda,
Ashley, Alyssa, Katherine,
Hannah, Karen, Susi, Gabi, and Sami.
May you always remember
who you are
and whose you are.
You are deeply loved by
the One who created you,
more than you will ever know.

From Alyssa:
To Jeff: Thank you for showing me
how God is the Relentless Lover
through your unending and gracious love.

To my mentors: Mom, Amy,
Dani, Robin, Jill, and Jeri.
Thank you for teaching and showing me
that we are spoken for
and that his love is truly
the greatest of all.

CONTENTS

■ ■ ■ ■

ONE:
AN EPIC LOVE
STORY — YOURS

■ ■ ■ ■

One bright April morning Alyssa and I (Robin) were busy in my kitchen preparing food for a youth event at church. All the windows were open. A gentle breeze cooled us. The television was on in the background, but we weren't paying much attention. I reached for the remote to turn it off but accidentally changed the channel.

"Oh, wait," Alyssa said. "Leave it there. I love this part."

I had happened upon an oldie-but-goodie chick flick at just the right moment. It was one of my favorites too. Alyssa and I stopped what we were doing. We stood together in a sweet silence and watched as the fair maiden ran into the arms of her hero. We sighed and looked at each other. Alyssa had tears in her eyes. So did I. We pointed at each other and laughed. "Why are we crying?" I asked. "I'm sure we've both seen this a dozen times."

"I know," Alyssa said wistfully. "But it's such a great love story. And love stories get me every time."

It's true, isn't it? Love stories draw us in. Honestly, who doesn't love a good love story? The pursuit. The suspense. The drama. The mystery. We cry, we laugh, we cheer — all for love. We are captivated by our favorite movies, television shows, and books when the romantic elements capture our imaginations and enliven our hopes.

Even if you don't see yourself as a girlie girl and didn't have a favorite Disney princess when you were growing up, you know in your core that you want to be loved like the heroines in all the best films and stories. You want to see love conquer all.

The desire to be loved, cherished, and adored never goes away. All of us long to believe someone is out there who wants us. Someone who will come for us. Someone who will take the role of the hero in our lives and love us, deeply love us, not for what we do or how we look but simply for who we are.

What if you could know that you *are* loved that intensely? You *are* sought after. You *are* the bride-to-be in a love story that's unfolding in your life right this minute. You are spoken for.

This love story began once upon a time long ago before you were even born. Almighty God, the Creator of the galaxies, thought of *you*. He carefully fashioned *you* — your voice, your fingers, your mind, even every one of your eyelashes. He carefully and deliberately crafted you. For all time there only has been and only will be one of you.

He saw all your days before you took your first breath. He knows all your thoughts before you speak them. He knows everything about you. From the very beginning you were known, and you were wanted. He is pursuing you like a tenacious bridegroom with a perfect proposal. He has set his affections on you. Why? Because he loves you, and he will never stop loving you. You are his first love, and he wants you back.

How do you respond to such unwavering, unending, unstoppable love?

In this book we will unwrap the ancient truths from God's Word about what it means to be loved, to be sought after, to be spoken for. You will see how the Bible is a love letter written to us. Through that love letter God makes it clear that he desires to be with us forever. Alyssa and I will share details from forever-love stories and show

how our love for God grew as he pursued us.

Our goal is simple. We want you to see what happens when you respond to the invitation of the true Bridegroom and step into the center of an epic love story — yours.

■ ■ ■ ■

Two:
You Are Wanted

■ ■ ■ ■

Embedded in our souls is a quiet wish, a secret hope we carry with us always.

We want to feel wanted.

Yet we struggle to fit in and to be included. It's more common to experience rejection than acceptance. We're more familiar with the bitter sting of being left out than with the delight of being sought out. All of us know what it's like to be overlooked and unwanted.

When was the last time you felt that way?

Was it last week when a group of friends decided to get together and none of them thought to include you? Or was it last month when you poured your heart out to a guy who expressed interest in you, only to find out that he didn't share any of your romantic feelings?

Perhaps the ache of feeling unwanted hit hardest when you were a child. You over-heard your parents fighting and came to the conclusion that your presence on planet Earth was an inconvenience to them.

Or maybe more recently you were caught off guard when you applied for the ideal job. You waited days for the call. After convincing yourself you would be hired, you were told in an impersonal way that the position had been filled. You were not wanted.

Yes, we all know the wrenching pain that comes from experiencing rejection. Our hopes are crushed, our feelings ignored, our hearts broken. What do we do? We pull back. We draw inward and give way to doubt and distrust. We brace ourselves against further hurt, and with a straight face we say that we don't care. It doesn't matter. No one can hurt us.

And yet . . .

The longing to be wanted continues to be the cry of our hearts. We dream of being sought out, included, welcomed, and warmly embraced. But living as we do in the rubble of a fallen world, rejection, not acceptance, seems most often to accompany us on our life journey.

So why do we keep hoping? Why does the secret wish to be wanted never go away? The hope lingers over us like a lullaby because we were created to experience love and to give love. We were made to belong, to be accepted, to be included. We were created to be in community with God and with others. He has reached out to us so that we might know *who* we are and *whose* we are.

You see, you were bought at a great price. You belong to the One who made you. You are spoken for. Almighty God, your heavenly Father, will never leave you, never reject you, and never say "Go away." He moved heaven and earth to make known to you this steadfast truth: you *are* wanted.

Robin

The worst rejection I ever experienced came when I was twenty-one.

I was engaged to a guy I'd met in college. I thought we had done everything right. We were friends first, dated in group settings at the Christian college we attended, and waited until after he graduated before we became engaged.

Then one February afternoon he looked me in the eye and spoke words that broke my heart: "I can't marry you. I don't love you. I don't want to spend the rest of my life with you."

My wedding dress was hanging in the closet. The invitations had been selected. In a single moment I went from believing I

21

was loved and wanted to being told I was not wanted. I was very much unloved.

He went on to reveal big pieces of his life that he had kept hidden from me. I was not his one and only. I was, in his opinion, absurdly romantic to have written letters to my future husband declaring my loyalty to him and praying for his faithfulness to me. My unrealistic expectations, he said, had caused our relationship to fail.

I will never forget how that rejection felt. I was so confused.

For days I tried to make sense of it. I struggled to separate the truth from the lies. Acidic thoughts kept me awake at night. *The problem is me. It is. That's why he ended our engagement. I'm too idealistic, like he said. I put too much pressure on him when I gave him the letters I'd written to my future husband. If I hadn't romanticized our relationship, we'd still be together.*

A destructive cycle of thinking kicked in. I thought that if I worked hard to make improvements in my personality, my body shape, my looks, and especially my beliefs, then he would want me again. I would be accepted by him, and we could be together. He would take me back. He would love me again if only I would change. I *had* to change.

Yet it soon became clear that none of my efforts would change his heart. He had made his final decision, and I was out of his life for good.

Not to mention that none of the changes I might attempt would be lasting, because they wouldn't be true to who I was and what I believed. Temporary adjustments to please him wouldn't alter who I was at the core. Eventually my true personality, opinions, and values would come through.

The raw and horrible truth was that I was unwanted. Cast aside. Unloved.

The only thing — and I do mean the only thing — that kept my heart above water in the wake of that life-altering rejection was that I knew, really truly knew, Someone wanted me. Someone who took me in just the way I was. Someone who had already invited me to be his bride. My relationship with him was sealed for eternity. He was my way out of the hurt. He was the One who spoke truth to me. He was the One who showed me true love.

That Bridegroom was Jesus. He loved me. He wanted me. Always.

My journey with Christ began when I was twelve years old and went to summer church camp. My main objective during that week was to be included in the popular group. I wanted to share the inside jokes and be invited to hang out at the camp pool with my new best friends. I dearly wanted to be wanted.

My efforts met with success, and by the last night I was sitting in the front row with the most popular kids at camp. I even knew the clever hand motions the group had made up to go along with the songs. It felt great being on the inside.

Acquiring that favored position had taken a lot of work, but it came with a fleeting reward. In the morning when camp ended, all of us would go our separate ways. I remember feeling sad that our gang was going to be dismantled.

Then the speaker said something that grabbed my attention: "God doesn't have any grandchildren. Just because your parents are Christians, that doesn't automatically make you a Christian."

What got to me was the way the speaker explained that God doesn't show us favor because we're part of an insiders' group. He doesn't give us special consideration because of our families. He invites us to come to him as individuals. And that night I did. I responded with my whole heart to receive Jesus Christ as my Savior and Lord.

If anyone would have asked me prior to

that last night at camp if I was a Christian, I would have said yes. I'd grown up going to church, so of course I was a Christian. It seemed to me the same as if someone had asked me if I were an American after having lived in the United States my whole life.

But I had never personally responded to the invitation to enter God's forever family. My prayer that night was simple. I knew that I could never be good enough through my own efforts to be right and pure before God. I needed to receive the gift of Christ's sacrifice. I needed to ask God to forgive all my sins.

My camp counselor prayed with me that night, and I calmly surrendered my life to Christ. As soon as I looked up at her, big, sloshy tears streamed down my face. I was overwhelmed to realize that God wanted me. He loved me. He wanted me to be in a close relationship with him. He promised he would never leave me. He would never give up on me. He accepted me into his kingdom. I felt so loved. So wanted.

The first thing I did after summer camp was start to read my Bible. I remember one day reading somewhere in the middle of 1 John and feeling as if I was reading a love letter. That's when I made the heart-pounding discovery that the Bible is a love story, an epic love story, in which every page is laced with evidence of God's unending love for us.

> See what great love the Father has
>   lavished on us!
>   1 John 3:1

For years after that night, I read God's Word and memorized his promises and eternal truths. Some days during my time alone with God, I felt as if I were on a treasure hunt, searching for the nuggets of truth that applied to what I was going through at the time.

That's how the Bible touched my heart right after my fiancé ended our engagement. I remember opening my Bible and my heart fully to the Lord. I felt so raw and vulnerable. I was looking for comfort, and I found it. Throughout God's beautiful love letter, I discovered reassuring evidence of his unfailing love. I started a list of verses and titled it "What God Says About You."

Whenever I felt discouraged about what my ex-fiancé or others said about me, I went to the list of what God said about me and found my heart filling up with life-giving hope. I even found a verse, John 3:29, in which John the Baptist referred to Jesus as the "bridegroom" and those who followed him as his "bride." His Word healed me. I knew that no matter what happened with any other relationship, Jesus would always want me.

A few years later I met the man who is now my husband. My heart was anchored, and I was much more prepared for marriage because I understood more fully what it meant for Jesus to be my First Love. My hopes were realistic because they were founded in his truth.

I also discovered that I *was* realistic to hope for faithfulness and to grow in a relationship that was flooded with the light of God's truth and forgiveness. Even though my letters to my future husband had been given away and never returned, the man I did marry was the answer to the prayers I had written from my hopelessly romantic heart when I was a teenager.

I encourage you to take some time alone with God to go through the list of "What God Says About You" at the end of this chapter. Look up the verses, and mark your favorite ones in your Bible. Soak up the truth of how deeply God loves you and how much he wants you. Believe me when I say that the anchor of God's truth will keep you steady through every stormy relationship.

So I want you to realize that the LORD
your God is God. He is the faithful God.
He keeps his covenant for all time to
come. He keeps it with those who love
him and obey his commands. He shows
them his love.
— Deuteronomy 7:9, NIrV

Alyssa

Just like Robin, I discovered how much God loves me when I was a teenager. I also discovered how painful it can be when you realize you are not wanted.

My freshman year in high school was a season of big changes. I'd graduated junior high, surrendered my life to Jesus, started high school, formed new friendships, and experienced my first real love. (Big changes, people, big changes!)

Now, I had had crushes in the past. Oh boy, did I have crushes! But *this,* this was the real deal. This boy was different. He and I would talk forever. E-mailed each other. Served with each other in our youth group. He was the first boy I knew who really loved Jesus. He was the first boy who made me want to love Jesus and seek him more. This guy pointed me to God, and I was in love.

Yes, I was in love with Jesus but also in love with this guy. I spent hours thinking about him and our possible future together. My best friend and I would stay up until the wee hours talking about the boys we liked. We would analyze every conversation and every thought and anxiously wait for those guys to pursue us. Oh, how desperately I wanted to be with this guy. How much I wanted him to want me too and to choose me.

However, as the months wore on, instead of my dream coming true, he and I were growing further and further apart. He gave no indication he liked me. He never pursued me and never called to hang out, as I had so hoped. No, he didn't want me. I wasn't his choice. He was a great guy and definitely a friend, but he didn't reciprocate my feelings.

I can't tell you how many nights I cried myself to sleep. How many prayers I prayed. My heart was broken.

Until one night I finally gave up. I gave it all to the Lord — my heart, my dreams, my longings, and this guy. I was done. I couldn't bear the rejection anymore. I asked God to take over and mend my heart. To show me his unfathomable love and how *he* wants me. I didn't heal overnight. The feelings didn't go away immediately, and the loneliness and hurt still stung. But slowly the

Lord revealed himself to me. Slowly the Lord showed me how deeply he loved and cherished me, how he was ultimately the Love of my life. And slowly the Lord helped me to move on. Yes, it took years. But the Lord was faithful to walk through those years with me — years of constant surrender and trusting his best for my life.

The summer before my freshman year I had started my relationship with Jesus. No big moment happened. No altar call occurred. Instead, I was bored one day and decided to read a book my mom had bought me, one in the Christy Miller Series by Robin Jones Gunn. I hadn't met Robin yet, so to me it was just a teen romance, but I later learned it was the first novel Robin had written for teen girls.

On those pages I found a friend, Christy — a fifteen-year-old girl who comes to know Jesus. Not just know about Jesus or all the facts about Jesus, but actually comes to know *him.*

This fictional character's life changed after that decision. She fell in love with God, the One who had wanted her so much that he sent his Son to die on the cross for her sins.

Yes, this beautiful Savior transformed Christy's life. Everything changed for her.

I desperately wanted to know, adore, and

live for Jesus like Christy did. Through her example I was ushered into a forever relationship with God.

But it wasn't until my freshman year, when I walked through my season of love, disappointment, loneliness, and hurt, that I truly understood Jesus's love for me. Whether I was wanted by a boy or not, Jesus wanted me. *Jesus.* He loves me. He likes me! He wants to be with me, and no sin, no barrier of time or space, would stop him from winning my heart.

It's the same with you.

He wants you.

No matter if you're single, dating, married, or ninety-nine years old, Jesus wants you. He is after your heart. I don't think I would have understood that beautiful truth as deeply if I hadn't walked through my season of rejection.

Robin and I aren't the only ones who know the sting of rejection. Throughout life we'll all experience many kinds of loss and hurt. The opinions and actions of others do not define us. We are known and wanted by the Lord himself. He never changes, never turns on us, never gives up on us.

All the fiery pain from rejection by other people can be put into perspective when you know that you are wanted by the Bridegroom. He made the stars. He tells the sun when to rise each morning. His hand holds back the ocean. His faithfulness endures for a thousand generations. He made you. He wants you. He loves you.

The lies, the memories of past hurts, the ache of rejections — those things burrow deep in our hearts, and most of us spend a lot of time digging those hurtful experiences back up. Whatever your story, whatever pain and hurt you have experienced, God knows. Not only does he know, but he has entered into your story. He has made a way for you to know your Savior, your Healer, your King. He wants to heal you, to make you like his Beloved Son, and to be with you forever. No, this life won't be pain free. But Jesus promises to walk with us through the pain. He never leaves. Ever. He is our Rock.

We will never fully understand why God allows us to go through pain and trials, but one reason is to draw us to him. When we walk through a trial, if we turn to him as our refuge and comfort, regardless of how messy and doubtful we may be, he draws us close into his embrace. He welcomes us in. He showers us with his love.

This is an epic love story that you are part of. You are wanted. Draw in that eternal truth: You. Wanted. Forever.

Come walk with us as we see how God woos each of us into a beautiful love story that will change our lives.

But the LORD longs to show you his favor.
He wants to give you his tender love.
— Isaiah 30:18, NIrV

WHAT DO YOU THINK?

1. Describe a time when you were wanted and what that felt like.

2. Think about a time you were left out or rejected. How did you handle the hurt?

3. How do you think God feels as he waits for us to come to him?

4. If you have given your life to Christ, recall what that moment was like for you.

5. If you haven't made the decision to enter into a relationship with Christ, the Bridegroom, you can do that by praying a simple prayer to invite him into your heart. Why not do so right now? It will be the beginning of your epic love story.

- You were made in my image (Genesis 1:27).
- You are my treasured possession, my peculiar treasure (Exodus 19:5, NIV, KJV).
- If you seek me with your whole heart, you will find me (Deuteronomy 4:29).
- When you are brokenhearted, I am close to you (Psalm 34:18).
- Delight in me, and I will give you the desires of your heart (Psalm 37:4).
- I know everything about you (Psalm 139:1).
- I know when you sit down and when you stand up (Psalm 139:2).
- I am familiar with all your ways (Psalm 139:3).
- I knit you together when you were in your mother's womb (Psalm 139:13).
- You are fearfully and wonderfully made (Psalm 139:14).
- All your days were written in my book before there was one of them (Psalm 139:16).
- My thoughts toward you are as countless as the grains of sand on the seashore (Psalm 139:17–18).
- As a shepherd carries a lamb, I have carried you (Isaiah 40:11).

- I knew you before you were conceived (Jeremiah 1:5).
- My plans for your future are for good, to give you hope (Jeremiah 29:11).
- I have loved you with an everlasting love (Jeremiah 31:3).
- I will never stop being good to you (Jeremiah 32:40).
- I will take pleasure in doing good things for you and will do those things with all my heart and soul (Jeremiah 32:41).
- I want to show you great and marvelous things (Jeremiah 33:3).
- I rejoice over you with singing (Zephaniah 3:17).
- I am your provider. I will meet all your needs (Matthew 6:31–33).
- I know how to give good gifts to my children (Matthew 7:11).
- I gave you the right to become my child when you received my Son, Jesus, and believed in his name (John 1:12).
- I am the Bridegroom and you are my bride (John 3:29).
- I have prepared a place for you. I will come back for you and take you to myself so that we can be together forever (John 14:3).
- I love you even as I have loved my only

Son (John 17:23).
- I revealed my love for you through Jesus (John 17:26).
- I determined the exact time of your birth and where you would live (Acts 17:26).
- In me you live and move and have your being (Acts 17:28).
- I am for you and not against you (Romans 8:31).
- I will never allow anything to separate you from my love for you (Romans 8:35–39).
- I gave my Son so that you and I could be reconciled (2 Corinthians 5:19).
- I am your peace (Ephesians 2:14).
- I am able to do more than you could possibly imagine (Ephesians 3:20).
- I am at work in you, giving you the desire and the power to fulfill my good purpose for you (Philippians 2:13).
- I did not give you a spirit of fear but of power, love, and self-discipline (2 Timothy 1:7).
- Every good gift you receive comes from my hand (James 1:17).
- I desire to lavish my love upon you because you are my child and I am your Father (1 John 3:1).
- My love for you is not based on your

love for me (1 John 4:10).
- I gave the ultimate expression of my love for you through Jesus (1 John 4:10).
- I am the complete expression of love (1 John 4:16).
- I will dwell with you in heaven. You will be mine, and I will be your God (Revelation 21:3).
- I will one day wipe away every tear from your eyes, and there will be no more crying or pain or sorrow (Revelation 21:4).
- I have written your name in my book (Revelation 21:27).
- I invite you to come (Revelation 22:17).

■ ■ ■ ■

THREE:
YOU ARE PURSUED

■ ■ ■ ■

Have you ever been pursued? Not in a creepy, stalker sort of way but in a good way, like being selected for a job or to be included in an exclusive group or by someone who wanted to have a close relationship with you.

It's humbling and even thrilling to know someone thinks you're worth snatching up.

God's way of pursuing us is by patiently drawing us to him. His love letter is laced together with beautiful, soul-stirring evidence that we humans are the object of his affection. He wants us to be his.

One of the strongest declarations of how God feels about us is in Jeremiah 31:3: "I have loved you with an everlasting love; therefore I have drawn you with lovingkindness" (NASB).

This verse stirs up a reminder of what happened in the Garden of Eden after Adam and Eve disobeyed. God didn't destroy them on the spot. He didn't turn his back on them and ignore them. He pursued them. He drew them out of hiding and provided for their needs.

Adam and Eve were the first to experience the tender ways of God, the Relentless Lover. Because we were made for him, he never stops pursuing us. We are his, and he wants us back.

Alyssa

I've found it easier to understand God's patient, faithful love for me when I think about the way Jeff set his affections on me and pursued a relationship with me.

Our love story began a few years ago when I was twenty-two. Some close girlfriends and I were gathered in a circle on the floor of the church auditorium, enjoying our fast-food burgers. We were giddy with excitement because one of our friends was getting married the next day.

From the other side of the circle a friend said, "Lyss, I know a boy who is smitten with you."

My heart beat a little faster. My hands felt sweaty. Did I hear right? A boy was smitten with me? How could that be? I had been gone from my hometown in Washington State for three years at college and was just

44

home for two weeks before I left for an internship on Maui. Who lived in the area that would have a crush on me when I hadn't even been around?

Her grin grew wider. I gave a little laugh so no one would know that inwardly I was freaking out. I had to ask, "So, who is it?"

"Jeff Bethke!"

"Jeff Bethke? I hardly know him."

"He knows who you are. We've had your senior photo on our fridge since high school. Over the last few months every time he comes over he looks at your picture longingly and asks when you're coming home."

"Really?" I was shocked. Jeff and I had had a few Facebook interactions, but that was about it.

"Yeah," my friend added, "my brother and I are always telling him how great you are. He's dying to meet you."

All I could do was smile. Deep down I was flattered. But I couldn't put much hope in meeting Jeff, let alone starting some sort of relationship with him. I was leaving in a week, and I'd be gone for two years.

In the past I had liked guys as a result of hearsay, but it never worked out. I had never dated before, and let me tell you, hearing that Jeff Bethke might have a crush on me threw me for a loop! Dating wasn't even on my radar, especially dating a guy I had never met in person before. (A few interactions online don't reveal the full scope of a person, no matter how much Facebook skimming one does!) No, I was better off dreaming that God had a surfer husband waiting for me on Maui.

The next day my friend's wedding was beautiful. Like I do at all weddings, I cried. Tears of joy, sweet joy. I was so excited for my friend. But I was also shaking all over because I had heard that Jeff was at the wedding too. He told my friend he wanted to meet me.

Freak. Out.

Toward the end of the reception, Jeff came over to the table where I sat, pulled up the chair next to me, and began to talk. My stomach did flips.

Right away I knew this guy was different. He didn't start in with small talk. He went directly into what God was doing in his life, how he had been saved, how he loved Jesus. He asked me questions that drew me out and showed he cared.

As we talked, I became convinced this guy was special. He captured my heart.

I wouldn't say it was love at first sight. I mean, the dude was handsome, but I had my guard up because I hardly knew him.

Jeff and I had one week from the wedding to the day we both left — me to Maui and Jeff to Oregon for college. Jeff pursued me all week, conspiring with his buddies to figure out ways he and I could hang out. On the day after the wedding, he asked if I wanted to go to church in Seattle with him and his two best friends. I was intrigued by Jeff, so I gladly went. During the drive we rocked out to Taylor Swift and Disney tunes. Seriously!? This was my dream man. (What I didn't know until a couple of years later was that Jeff blew out his car speaker that night trying to impress me, and he had downloaded those songs because he knew they were my favorites.)

The last night we were together, his best friend had a good-bye party for Jeff, and I was invited. We had a blast, roasting marshmallows and hanging out. What I didn't know then was that the whole group was plotting to put us together.

At one point everyone went inside, leaving Jeff and me by the fire. Jeff went deep, telling me more about his testimony and background. He was roasting three marshmallows over the fire as he was talking but then realized they were on fire. He brought them up close to his mouth to blow out the flames when those gooey suckers splatted right in his lap. Jeff dropped the stick and frantically tried to wipe the gooey, on-fire marshmallows off his lap, only to smear them all over his shorts and hands. He excused himself to change his shorts as I held back my giggles. Way to impress a girl, right? He came back after a few minutes, having doused himself in cologne. Oh yes, this guy was definitely into me!

I stayed as late as I could, hoping that Jeff would say something about staying in touch. Finally I had to leave, so I said my goodbyes. Everyone looked at Jeff. I stood up to walk away, when Jeff stood up quickly and sputtered out, "Alyssa, do you have a phone?" (Nervous much!?)

"Yes, I do."

"Um, can I have your number? I'd love to stay in touch while you're in Maui."

Finally. I gave him my number and walked to my car with a huge smile on my face. Oh yes, I wanted to stay in touch with Jeff Bethke.

Over the next couple of months, he called me a few times, and each phone call lasted several hours. The more we talked, the more my heart melted for him. This guy was a true God lover. He was real, honest, smart, funny, and sensitive. We could talk for hours, and it was like no time passed.

Jeff continued to pursue me and to initiate the relationship. After a few months he asked me to be his girlfriend, and we began dating long-distance. He was my first boyfriend. I was giddy. Over the moon. Glowy.

As much I'd hoped and dreamed that an amazing guy like Jeff would be interested in me one day, I couldn't believe it was actually happening. Jeff's deliberate pursuit of me led me to understand what it feels like when God pursues us. Jesus truly has his eye on us. He tenderly, patiently shepherds us and draws us to himself.

> Bless those who belong to you.
> Be their shepherd. Take care of them
>   forever.
>   — Psalm 28:9, NIrV

Robin

Alyssa and I met by God's divine happenstance. She was serving a two-year internship at a church on Maui when my husband and I moved to the island. Alyssa and I became instant forever friends. She told me how God had used the Christy Miller books I had written years earlier to play a significant role in her relationship with the Lord. From there we discovered that we both loved communicating with young

49

women and shared a romantic heart when it came to our relationships with Christ.

One afternoon we met to plan an event for the high school girls at church. The day was so glorious that we decided to conduct our business on the beach. We took a refreshing dip in the deep blue before planning the high school gathering.

Somewhere in the conversation I used the term *Relentless Lover* to describe the way I viewed God's pursuit of us.

"How did you come up with that description?" Alyssa asked.

I told her about a radio interview I had more than fifteen years ago. In most interviews I'm asked questions such as "Where do you get the ideas for your stories?" or "What prompted you to write for teens?" This interview, however, kicked off with a startling question.

I had walked into the studio and put on the headset. Then the interviewer looked at me and said, "So, how can you call yourself a Christian and write romance novels?"

We were on the air! Live! People were listening! And everyone, including me, was waiting for how I was going to answer.

"Well . . ."

The words tumbled out before I had time to consider them. "I think the reason is because when I was a teenager, I read a love story that changed my life."

"A love story?"

"Yes. The relationship starts off well. Actually, very well. And then in the first few chapters everything falls apart. You think they are never going to get back together, but you hope they will, so you keep reading. About three-fourths of the way through the book, he does everything he can to prove his love to her. But still she won't come back to him. Then in the last chapter, he rides in on a white horse and takes her to be with him forever."

The host looked at me skeptically. "How could a book like that change your life? It sounds like a formula romance novel to me."

"Really, a formula romance?"

"Yes. Isn't that what you were talking about?"

"Actually I was talking about the Bible."

"The Bible?"

"Yes. The love story I read as a teenager was the Bible. There's a white horse and everything."

The radio host pulled back and stared at me. For a moment the radio station experienced what no on-air host ever wants — dead air.

"We're going to cut to a station break, and

then we'll be right back." The host pushed a few buttons and looked at me, stunned, before saying off the air, "You are absolutely right. I never saw that before. The Bible is the ultimate love story."

"God even calls us his bride," I added.

"You're right. He does."

We went back on the air, and I said, "I think God is the Relentless Lover, and we are his first love. That's why he never stops pursuing us. He's not a vengeful God who wants to 'get back at us'; he's a patient, loving God who wants to 'get *us* back.' "

> Then I saw heaven opened, and behold, a white horse! The one sitting on it is called Faithful and True, and in righteousness he judges and makes war.
> — Revelation 19:11, ESV

The rest of the hourlong interview zipped along with more lively conversation about what it looks like when God, the Relentless Lover, pursues us, his first love.

Evidence of that relentless pursuit is found in the beginning of the Bible. Genesis 3:8 says that Adam and Eve "heard the sound of the LORD God as he was walking in the garden in the cool of the day." Adam and Eve had just sinned by eating the forbidden fruit. Everything that was beautiful in their lives was now broken, including their relationship with God. Yet notice how, even in that painful moment of God's confronting them about their poor choice, the description of that encounter has a romantic sound to it. They heard the sound of the Lord God. He was walking toward them in the cool of the day. He wasn't stomping or charging at them. He was walking toward them to initiate reconciliation.

This isn't the image of a fierce, omniscient power wrathfully flinging lightning bolts, prepared to release his fury on the two rebellious souls. No, this is the sound and image of a broken-hearted Creator pursuing the man he had handcrafted so meticulously from the earth's dust. This is the Giver of Life pursuing the woman he had sculpted so precisely from Adam, for Adam.

This is the Relentless Lover tenderly coming to redeem that which was lost.

He was the One doing the pursuing from the beginning. And he still is today. Right now.

Learn to listen until you recognize the sound of the Lord God walking in the garden of your heart. He's coming for you, drawing you to him because he loves you and wants to be with you.

Let's recognize him as the LORD.
Let's keep trying to really know him.
You can be sure the sun will rise.
And you can be just as sure the LORD will
  appear.
He will come to renew us like the winter
  rains.
He will be like the spring rains that water
  the earth.

— Hosea 6:3, NIrV

The amazing thing about God's unfailing kindness is that he hasn't given up on his creation, us, for thousands of years. Some people delayed nearly a lifetime before responding to the Relentless Lover. They ignored all the nudges, all the whispers, all the times God made it clear that he wanted to be their God. Instead, those stubborn souls kept thinking they could do life on their own without God, even though he is the One who created them. They decided they could handle all their problems without calling on him for wisdom and direction, which he promises to give freely and generously to all who ask.

That concept touched me deeply a few months ago when I came across Genesis 6:6. As a matter of fact, when I read it, I unexpectedly burst into tears.

I'd read that verse many times over the years, but I'd not paid any special attention to it before. This time the verse went deep inside me.

It appears at the beginning of the account of Noah and the ark. Little more than fifteen hundred years had passed since God created Adam and Eve and placed them in the Garden of Eden. During that time most everyone on earth had moved further and further away from God. Very few sought him. Even fewer honored him. Wickedness and violence dominated the planet. None of the good things God had designed for Adam and Eve was being enjoyed.

Genesis 6:5 says that every intent of humanity's heart was "only evil continually" (NASB).

How tragic! God had created a perfect world and given Adam and Eve the freedom to choose to obey or disobey him. When they chose disobedience, that mind-set toward God continued generation after generation. Every intent of their hearts was only evil continually.

The next verse is the one that made me cry. It simply says, "The LORD was sorry that He had made man on the earth, and He was grieved in His heart" (Genesis 6:6, NASB).

My heart ached for God. More than a thousand years of continual rejection. More than a thousand years of patiently pursuing a relationship with the people he had created. But virtually no one wanted him. That loss of relationship grieved his heart, and he was sorry he had made us.

I cried that day because I don't ever want God to be sorry that he made me. I don't ever want him to be grieved in his heart because of me.

Even though God never stops pursuing us and it's never too late to turn to him, none of us knows how many minutes we have left on earth. Jesus even said that, as it was in the days of Noah, so it will be when he returns. No one knows the hour or the day (Matthew 24:36–39).

Let's not be among those who presume on God's goodness and think we have all the time in the world to run off in our own direction and then call out to God to save us at the last minute. He has been pursuing you since before you were born. Stop and turn to him. Let him catch you.

Today is a very good day to start fresh as a woman who knows who she is and whose she is. You are a princess in God's kingdom. One day the Prince of Peace will come riding in on a white horse because he wants to take you to be with him forever. All the fairy tales that were ever dreamed up come from this one true tale. God's story. A story he wants to write throughout your life.

"Sing and rejoice, O daughter of Zion! For behold, I am coming and I will dwell in your midst," says the LORD.
— Zechariah 2:10, NKJV

1. How do you view the Bible? How does that view shift if you think of it as a love letter written to you?

2. In what ways can you relate to Alyssa's hesitation to believe that someone was smitten with her?

3. Describe a time when you felt God was pursuing you or drawing you closer to him.

4. How did you feel when you read Genesis 6:6 about God being sad that he had made humankind?

5. What sort of expression do you imagine on the face of Jesus, the Prince of Peace, when he comes for you on a white horse?

■ ■ ■ ■

FOUR:
YOU ARE LOVED

■ ■ ■ ■

Jesus loves me, this I know, for the Bible tells me so.

Did you sing that familiar song as a child? How easy it was to believe those simple words when you were young. How comforting to sing it over and over when you were filled with all kinds of hope and a sense of wonder at life.

And then you grew up.

Right?

The simple, innocent faith you had in God and the trust you had in his love for you were rocked when you were exposed to the reality about human nature. Someone hurt you. Something you were counting on fell from your grasp. Terrible thoughts leaked into your imagination. Life became complicated. You became more complex. You tried to sort out the good from the bad, the truth from the lies. Your personal hunt for true love began, and the search was much more elaborate than the elemental foundation "Jesus loves me, this I know."

How is it possible to believe again with simple, childlike faith that Jesus really loves you?

Robin

I'd be the first to say that the answer to that question lies in the second line of the song: the Bible still tells us so. God's one Book is filled with declarations of his love. His Word is true. He keeps all his promises. Nothing has changed about God or his Word.

We are the ones who have changed.

As you look back over your life and all the experiences you've had, I'm guessing you could point to a collection of cuts, bruises, and scars that came from hurts, betrayals, disappointments, and loss. Those wounds are keeping you from believing that God really loves you.

Someone might tell you with confidence and passion that God is your heavenly Father and that he will never leave you because he loves you, but if your earthly father left you, it's difficult to believe your heavenly Father would be any different.

If you read in God's Word that Jesus called his disciples "friends" and that he promised to be with them until the end of the earth, you might think it sounds too good to be true. Why? Because you had a best friend who promised to always be there for you, but now the two of you no longer speak to each other.

You may have memorized a verse that filled your heart with peace because it gave you assurance that Almighty God was faithful and true and wanted only the best for you. But then someone you relied on turned out to be unfaithful and not true to his or her word. In the end that person only wanted what was best for him or her, not what was best for you.

As the list of life experiences grows, it's easy to doubt that love of any kind is real. Parental love, friendship love, romantic love — if someone has let you down in each of those relationships, your battered spirit has no place to put the simple truth that "Jesus loves me, this I know, for the Bible tells me so."

In the second chapter of this book, I shared how my confidence was crushed when I became disengaged and how I went to God's Word to learn all over again how much Jesus loves me. Part of the reason I needed God's perspective on how he saw me was because of the second wave of rejection that came during the months after the broken engagement.

Some couples joke, "So, who gets to keep our friends after we break up?" In our case my ex-fiancé kept pretty much all our mutual friends. I was quickly cut out of the loop and left off the guest lists for birthday parties and weddings. Every day on my social calendar was suddenly vacant. No plans. No invitations. Nothing but rejection on all sides.

In an effort not to become a hermit, I tried to connect with some of my old friends from high school. Finally I was included in a get-together at the home of a friend from my teen years. One of the guys at the gathering told me he attended the same church college group I went to. It was a large group, and even though we had noticed each other before, we had never met.

By the end of the party, he asked me out to coffee. It had been four months since the breakup, and I was ready for a date. I knew it was super casual and not even a real date, but someone was including me, and that felt good.

However, the next day he called to cancel. He said he would phone to reschedule, but he never did. Later I found out that rumors about me were making the rounds in my old circle of friends. I hadn't told any of my old friends the details of why the engagement ended. I guess that left a few of the creative ones in the group to come up with their own assumptions. It didn't matter that none of the gossip was true; it still destroyed my opportunity to reconnect with friends. What is also true is that gossip spreads like wildfire, destroying everything in its path.

Several girls in that group came to me privately looking for the inside scoop. I chose not to tell them the details. I wasn't sure at the time if that was a good idea because it resulted in a lot of alone time. But somehow it felt right not to share confidential details, even though the relationship was irreparably shattered. I sensed the girls were more interested in the dirt and the drama than they were in my feelings or my friendship.

During that time I learned something powerful about God's love. His love is not like human love. Not at all.

I realized that if I was going to understand the uniqueness and depth of God's love for me, I had to mentally separate my relationships with people from my relationship with the Lord. God's love should never be distorted or diminished by comparing it with the friendship or love of any human who has let me down, rejected me, betrayed me, or lied about me.

During that time my relationship with the Lord matured and grew deeper because I was learning to love him for who he was and not for what he did for me.

At just the right time, some girlfriends from church gathered around me, and those friendships deepened. Four of us took off that summer for a backpacking trip around Europe. We had the adventure of our lives. Every day we sensed God's closeness.

We had long talks on the trains and read the Bible to one another in the morning while dining on our continental breakfast of hard rolls and coffee at the youth hostels. At the same time I was discovering what a great big world this is, I was also learning that God was greater and more powerful than I'd ever imagined. He was not like anything else or anyone else. He alone was God.

It became clear that when I focused on the flawed love shown to me by humans and used that measurement to think about God's love, I was unwittingly making God human, but of course he isn't.

He is holy. He is almighty, all powerful, and all knowing, and he is love. We can't measure God by any love, friendship, compassion, or loyalty that we have ever known.

God is in a category all by himself. His love is true. He never changes. He is always faithful. Always patient. Always good. Always truthful. Always kind.

He loves us. Always.

Understanding God's love meant that I had to wrap my head around God's holiness. He is set apart from all humans.

> But set Christ apart as Lord in your hearts and always be ready to give an answer to anyone who asks about the hope you possess.
> — 1 Peter 3:15, NET

If you have found it difficult to believe that God's love is meant for you, start here: Set him apart in your heart. Separate what you know about God from what you know about everyone else who ever said he loved you or wanted to be with you forever or promised to be your friend. Don't compare God to any human. Humans fail. All of us do.

Jesus never fails. He is perfect. Always. In all things. At all times.

So when he says he loves you, that means he loves you.

Forever.

What does God's love for us look like?

How does it make us feel? Here's the definition of love that he gave us in 1 Corinthians 13:4–7: "Love is patient and kind. Love is not jealous or boastful or proud or rude. It does not demand its own way. It is not irritable, and it keeps no record of being wronged. It does not rejoice about injustice but rejoices whenever the truth wins out. Love never gives up, never loses faith, is always hopeful, and endures through every circumstance" (NLT).

Now read those verses again and think about how every one of those attributes of love is true of God and his love for you.

Without a doubt you are loved by God. You are eternally, extravagantly, tenderly loved. That truth has never changed, and it never will.

Jesus loves you, this you know. For the Bible tells you so.

Alyssa

Most of the time I dated Jeff, I was on cloud nine. Whenever his name was mentioned, I couldn't help but smile big. My heart melted every time I heard his voice on the phone or received a letter from him. I had fallen for this guy and fallen hard. However, our relationship was all long-distance, which didn't give either of us the full picture of who the other person was.

Even though we dated for a year, we only saw each other when I went home a couple of times and when Jeff flew out twice to see me in Hawaii. The last time he came to visit was for two weeks, which was the longest we had spent time together. In fact, the first week he was on Maui, my parents were visiting as well. The four of us stayed in a small condo — talk about a true act of love . . . I mean, the poor guy slept on the lumpy pull-out sofa.

The two weeks were wonderful. Hiking. Snorkeling. Cliff jumping. Serving together at church. He had a chance to see my life, parents, friends, church, job, roommates. However, since we hadn't spent much time together, I didn't understand any of his "Jeffisms." You know, what it meant when he was quiet. Or how he felt in group situations. Or how he interacted with my friends and family.

I misunderstood Jeff. I took his sometimes standoffishness as his choosing not to pursue me or cherish me. Instead, he was taking it all in and was a bit nervous. Would my friends like him? What did influential people in my life think of him?

I concluded that Jeff didn't like me, that he didn't cherish me as I so wanted him to.

If a guy likes you, shouldn't he bring you flowers and instantly know your favorite Starbucks drink? (Iced soy caramel macchiato, just in case you're wondering.) Shouldn't he want to see you at work or get to know the kids you work with? I thought cherishing a girl was evidenced by those things. I found out much later that those are nice but aren't the foundation of a relationship.

I also felt that this wasn't the right time for us to be together. We were in different seasons of life. He was in college across the ocean. I was done with college and living on a small island twenty-five hundred miles away. I couldn't envision our lives together.

So I broke up with him.

Over the next few months, I was left raw and pretty beat up. Breaking up with Jeff had broken me. I only vaguely understood why I was breaking up with him — I didn't feel cherished, and I couldn't see how our lives were going to come together. But I couldn't wrap my mind fully around why I had walked away from him. My heart was telling me I was over the moon about him, but my mind was saying he didn't totally love me and it wouldn't work out.

Looking back, I know that we needed to go our separate ways. God did amazing things in both of our lives the year we weren't dating.

However, there is no way around it: that summer was one of the hardest seasons of my life. I doubted God's goodness, and I feared his plan for my life. I questioned if God was good enough to ever bring a husband into my life. I was a shattered soul. I didn't want to admit to others that breaking up with Jeff had left me so heartbroken. I mean, *I* was the one to break up. I wanted to appear strong and put together when I was the exact opposite. I was weak, messy, and extremely vulnerable.

In September I started my second year of internship on Maui. I was matched up with a new mentor, and one afternoon as we were sitting in the open courtyard at church, she asked a question that caught me by surprise.

"Alyssa, do you really believe God loves you?"

My world stopped. My heartbeat quickened. Why was she asking me such a question?

Of course I believe God loves me. I mean, I know he loves me. That's what his Word says. But do I believe it? Wow, I don't know.

"I guess I wonder at times," I admitted.

She knew about my relationship with Jeff

and my heartache over breaking up with him. Having her ask me that poignant question, though, to say it so bluntly, caused me to search my heart.

What I came to learn during that next year was that God was for me. He is my portion. He is mine, and I am his. I get God. He's all I need. Really.

As crazy as it sounds, sometimes I want to go back to that summer — or entire year, really — because I've never been closer to the Lord. He met me in my pain. He held me. He cared for me. He was intimate. I learned that sometimes our Good Shepherd leads us through valleys to build up our muscles to climb the mountains. And he doesn't let us do it alone but walks with us the whole way, sometimes carrying us until we can walk again.

God proved faithful. He knew my heart's desires but also knew how I needed to let him fill my desires first before he placed anyone else into my life. I needed to see how God was enough — and more than I could ever dream of. Not that being content in God means he will bring a husband into your life; it's not an equation. But see, I had idolized marriage for so long that I needed the Lord to break me from placing it above him. I had thought (although I never would have admitted it) that once I was married, then I would be completely happy, then I could be content and satisfied. That summer the Lord tore down my idol and revealed that he alone was enough. He was my portion, and I was rich to have him.

Knowing and believing this truth didn't come overnight. It took all year for the reality to sink in. I remember one moment in which the Lord showed me his love as I was reading Genesis.

I had decided to study the first book of the Bible, and I remember reading through the story of Abram, Sarai, and Hagar. Sarai was unable to have children, and although God had promised her a child, she didn't wait on his timing but ran ahead and told Abram to sleep with her servant Hagar to have a child. So Abram did as his wife said, and sure enough, Hagar gave birth to a son. Sarai was infuriated and lashed out at Hagar, causing her to run away.

Can you imagine? Being forced to sleep with your lady's husband, getting pregnant, and then having her turn on you? I would be terrified too. But God met Hagar right where she was. He tenderly comforted her and told her to go back. Hagar called God the "One who sees."

The One who sees. This phrase has been

woven into my heart ever since I read Hagar's story in Genesis 16. I remember sitting on the couch with a pillow and my Bible on my lap and tears dripping from my face.

God sees me. He sees me right now. I thought God had forgotten about me. I thought he had forsaken me, had crushed my dream, and had forgotten about my heart's desire. No, not at all. God knew my heartache. He knew my desire to be married. He hadn't forgotten or turned his head. Rather, he was facing me, doing what was best for me by crushing my idol and drawing me close to him.

Thereafter, Hagar used another name to refer to the LORD, who had spoken to her. She said, "You are the God who sees me."
— Genesis 16:13, NLT

True love is choosing the highest good for the other person. God loved me so much that he did what was best for me — and for Jeff — and that was our breaking up for a season.

God's love is manifested in many ways. He thoughtfully handcrafted each of us. He gave his Son to die and rise again for us. He sends us the Spirit to dwell in us to comfort, help, teach, and lead us. He gave us his Word. He blesses us with friends and family to walk life together. We are created from community to community. He gives us breath. And he knows our hearts and shows us his love each day. We simply have to open our eyes to see it.

Do you believe that God loves you?

I mean, do you really believe he loves you? It's hard in our culture to know what real love is. I love my parents, and I love berry cobbler served in miniature Mason jars (what girl doesn't!?). But let's hope that the love for my parents is much stronger than my love for those sweet cobbler-filled Mason jars.

We're bombarded daily with messages of what love is that are contrary to what God says. Music, movies, television, and our friends and family show us that love is conditional and that love is all about us. It often can be translated as "You make me happy" because it's all about how other people make us feel. That kind of love is based on what they can do for us, and when they fail, show weakness, or don't "fill us up," we split.

That kind of love is based on emotion, which is scary because there's no security.

That's why we hear "Well, I just fell out of love" or "I don't have those feelings anymore, so it's over."

If we accept the meanings of love that our culture feeds us, we question whether God loves us.

But that's not true love. God's love is unending, unconditional, and free. It's not based on what we do or don't do. It's not based on who we are or aren't. It's not promised to us when we're "all good to go," but rather, as God makes clear in Romans 5:8, his love is lavished on us even while we are sinners. This love is based on God's character because he is love itself.

Robin told me once that "love is an unconditional commitment to an imperfect person." That's how God loves us.

God is love.
— 1 John 4:8

To fully absorb his love for you, you might need to start by choosing to believe that God actually *likes* you. He wants to spend time with you. He wants to hear your heart, your struggles, your joys and pains. He wants all of you. He's crazy about you.

In John 15:9 Jesus said, "Just as the Father has loved Me, I have also loved you; abide in My love" (NASB).

Let yourself fully take in this fixed, eternal truth: God loves you. Believe it. Store this truth deep in your heart. And when you have doubts or go through a storm, remember who God is. What he has done in the past. What his Word says. Ask others to pray with you and for you, that God would show you how deep his love is for you.

And I pray that Christ will be more and more at home in your hearts, living within you as you trust in him. May your roots go down deep into the soil of God's marvelous love; and may you be able to feel and understand, as all God's children should, how long, how wide, how deep, and how high his love really is; and to experience this love for yourselves, though it is so great that you will never see the end of it or fully know or understand it. And so at last you will be filled up with God himself.

— Ephesians 3:17–19, TLB

1. Do you see yourself as the object of God's affection? Why or why not?

2. Why do you think God would keep loving his children even though they rebel against him?

3. Even if another human has loved you deeply, in what ways do you see God's love for you as deeper still?

4. How can you separate your understanding of God's love from your understanding of and/or hurt over a human's love for you?

5. In what ways would your life be different if you lived each day in the confidence and security of God's love?

■ ■ ■ ■

FIVE:
YOU HAVE
BEEN CALLED

■ ■ ■ ■

We have a dilemma. We know God wants a relationship with us, we see how faithfully he pursues us, and we start to believe that he deeply loves us. But we are still bent on going our own direction, and we are unhappy.

Every human since Adam and Eve has had the same problem:

We want what we want when we want it,
but
when we get it,
we no longer want it.

Why is that?

It has a lot to do with understanding and embracing *who* we are and *whose* we are.

We were created to be in a dependent relationship with God and to rely on him for everything. Yet society tells us to be independent, self-sufficient, liberated individuals. Individuality is strength, the ads tell us. Create your own success. Go after what you want. Be fierce in doing whatever it takes to make your dreams come true.

Magazines show us images of aloof, detached models, and we gaze at them thinking, *Now this is beauty. Such control! Such power!* Our culture praises and rewards the supremacy of self-reliance.

Yet God has called us out of this world and in the opposite direction of our culture's value system. His Word gives us example after example of people who ran hard after the fleeting prize of fame, wealth, and power, and every one of those independent-minded individuals ended up empty and still wanting.

God's Word is also filled with stories of people who sought him and his standards in the midst of difficult times, perverse societies, and great opposition. History is punctuated by those who put God's kingdom first and lived according to his values. As Psalm 112:6 says, "Surely the righteous will never be shaken; they will be remembered forever." Their lives were blessed for eternity because they chose not to live according to the system of this world.

Seek the Kingdom of God above all else,
and live righteously, and he will give you
everything you need.
— Matthew 6:33, NLT

So, what does it mean to be called?

We have been called *out* of this world and its value system and invited *into* God's eternal kingdom. We belong to the One who made us, loves us, and knows what's best for us. That's why we will be happy only when we fix our hope and affections on his kingdom and all that is eternal.

The big question is, how do we do that?

It begins with a choice. Your choice.

Do you want what you want when you want it? Or do you want what God wants when he wants it?

Alyssa

When I broke up with Jeff, that was my choice but not his. And it was one of the most difficult decisions of my life. The thing was, I really liked him. Like heart-beats-a-little-faster, butterflies-in-the-tummy, smile-from-ear-to-ear, get-a-little-clumsy-when-he's-around, cloud-nine liked him.

This guy had me.

I wanted to marry him.

But, as I mentioned in the last chapter,

during the week he was visiting me on Maui, I thought he didn't care for me the way I cared for him. I had to work all that week, and I thought he would visit me every day at work to help out. Instead, he went hiking with the guy interns. At one point when I gently mentioned the big *M* word (*ahem,* marriage), he got uncomfortable and changed the subject. I had so many doubts. Did he really like me? Was he the right one for me? Could our lives blend together? Was he even interested in marriage eventually? Was he ready to lead me?

Looking back, I can see my expectations were too high and my desires weren't expressed. I kept all my hurts and questions inside. I didn't understand how Jeff operated, and I didn't try to see our time together through his eyes. As a result of my not expressing any of this to him, he left Maui thinking our long-distance relationship would continue as it had for the last year.

Of course, that's not what happened.

I kept thinking and praying about our relationship, and I was torn up. The day after he left, I headed out with twenty-five high schoolers on a two-week mission trip. There I was, waiting to board the plane, when I realized I needed to break up with

Jeff. I wasn't sure why since I liked him so much. But I knew that's what I was supposed to do.

But I couldn't do it yet.

For the next two weeks I was responsible for focusing on and leading those students, yet I was in deep pain, knowing that I needed to break up with Jeff. I cried buckets of tears. Buckets!

He was my first boyfriend, so not only did I feel as though I was losing a good friend and saying good-bye to a guy I really liked, but I also felt like my dream of ever getting married had died.

I didn't handle the actual breakup conversation well. Actually that's an understatement. It was awful. I was awful. I called him the day after I returned home. Immediately he could tell I wasn't myself.

I kept the call short. No emotion. No tears. No sadness. I just said, "Jeff, I have to break up with you."

He was stunned. He asked why, and I stammered a few sentences, none of which made sense. How could they? I didn't even fully understand myself.

Then the worst thing happened. Jeff cried.

He asked if there was any hope for us getting back together. I said no. It was done. Forever. And that was that. Good-bye. *Click*.

I still can't believe how emotionless I was on that call. I think it must have been because I had wept so much during the two weeks building up to the conversation that I didn't have anything left in me when I finally talked to him.

That call broke him. And it broke me. We've been told that the person who does the breaking up doesn't go through as much pain as the other person. So not true in our case. Jeff didn't know it, but I was left raw for months.

But after that heartbreaking summer ended and I started my second year as an intern, I began to heal. As I explained in the last chapter, I learned from Hagar's story that God sees me. He was shepherding me and showing me how persistently he had been pursuing me.

During that season of healing, another Jeff — "Surfer Jeff" — pursued me. (Just can't get away from those Jeffs.)

Surfer Jeff went to my church. He pursued me for a month before I gave in and agreed to date him. A couple of weeks later Jeff Bethke texted me. He said he wanted to Skype.

I agreed. Let me tell you, the conversation wasn't at all what I expected. He asked me to be his forever. With each sentence he poured out his heart. He had written a list of things to say. Sweet things that every girl longs to hear.

"Lyss, I love you."

"I want to marry you."

"I'll move to Maui to be with you."

"There's no one like you."

I didn't know what to do with such an outpouring of affection and tenderness. I had longed to hear Jeff say those things while we dated. Why was he telling me now?

He wanted me to be set apart from dating other guys so that my heart would be clear and ready for a lifelong relationship with him.

He paused and waited for me to reply. He wanted to hear that everything he felt about me was what I also felt for him.

Instead of affirming words of mutual love, I said, "Jeff, I just started dating someone else."

"Who?"

"Another Jeff."

He ranted and raved about how Surfer Jeff would never love me the way he loved me. He said that Surfer Jeff didn't know what I needed, but he did.

I was infuriated. He was passionately confrontational. But looking back, I love him for it. Jeff was *fighting for me.* He didn't just let me go. He took a stand and fought to win my heart even though I had turned my attention toward this new relationship. It was such a picture of how God doesn't give up on us. How he calls us out of the distractions of our lives into a deeper relationship with him. But I didn't see it that way at the time because I was focused on going a different direction. My dreams for my future were all about Surfer Jeff.

Months went by. Things were going pretty well. I was finishing my internship, figuring out life and relationships and what God wanted for my future. On Valentine's Day Surfer Jeff told me he loved me as we stood overlooking the ocean, with roses scattered all around us. It had taken me awhile, but I had begun to believe that Surfer Jeff and I could get married. My thoughts were leaning toward what our future would be like together.

Then late one night under a smirking Maui moon, Surfer Jeff broke up with me. Out of the blue. The whole time we had dated I had been the hesitant one. He was the one who had consoled me and confidently led me. Now he was standing before me, spilling out all his doubts along with a list of things he couldn't put up with any longer.

I remember going to Robin's house the next day and being so emotionally and physically exhausted I could hardly tell her what had happened. Robin and her husband told me to go to their guest room, close the door, climb into bed, and not leave until that pillow was soaked with all my tears. I fell into a deep sleep. When I woke up, I still felt pretty awful. Nothing seemed to make sense.

Two weeks later Jeff e-mailed me a short message, asking how I was doing. He had found out that my relationship with Surfer Jeff was over, but he didn't mention that. He just asked how I was doing. At the time I didn't want anything to do with any guy, let alone someone named Jeff.

Finally I decided to reply and told him briefly that Surfer Jeff had broken up with me. He responded immediately, expressing sympathy and care.

As the next month progressed, a bunch of e-mails flew back and forth between us. Jeff was nothing but kind and tender. He pointed me to Jesus. He forgave me for how awfully I had broken up with him and for the way I had treated him after the breakup. He showered me with love.

As we exchanged e-mails, my heart began to heal. I could see how beautifully Jeff loved me. I began to care deeply for him, and I realized I didn't want to be with anyone else.

Jeff had never stopped loving me. He had made his intentions clear when he called me. When I didn't respond with equal devotion, Jeff didn't stop loving me. Instead, he stepped back and waited out my choice to focus my heart not on him but on Surfer Jeff. But he never gave up. He waited. He prayed. He hoped. And then he stepped in when the opportunity came. Jeff never stopped pursuing me.

Our love story is unique and isn't what I would have written for myself, for us. In fact, it's so much better. And one of the things I appreciate most about our story is how it shows off Jesus. It's a perfect example of how Jesus makes his love for us clear and then fights for us even as he waits for us to return to him. How he calls us to be with him, not just once but over and over.

It's easy for us to choose to go in a direction that we think will bring us what we want. Yet that direction will turn into a dead end, like my relationship with Surfer Jeff did. All along God is waiting for us to choose his way and give our hearts to him.

Robin

The longer we walk with the Lord, the more we realize there will always be another Jeff. Someone or something that seems like the fulfillment of our deep longings will pop up at just the right moment. We find it easy to set our affections on that someone or that something while all along our heavenly Father is patiently wooing us, pursuing us, calling us to be his alone.

I remember the day Alyssa came over after her breakup with Surfer Jeff and how we sent her to the guest room for a private sobfest. Sometimes there is nothing anyone can say or do to ease the pain of a trampled spirit. You just need to cry your little heart out. I love how King David wrote in Psalm 56:8 that God puts all our tears in his bottle. Even in the darkest valleys of life, our Good Shepherd sees. He knows. He cares.

What I saw in Alyssa that sad day and what I still see in her life is a longing to choose God's best. She didn't get angry at God for the way things turned out with Surfer Jeff. Instead she turned fully to God and sought his direction and his will for whatever was next in her life. Alyssa made herself available to God, and he met her right where she was. I watched the days pass and could see how he was a tender Shepherd to her, leading her beside still waters and restoring her soul.

Healing, hope, and true happiness begin when we are available to God. Even when we are shattered and lost, there's no point in trying to run from him. He longs to pick us up and carry us in his arms. So if you need to bleat, little lamb, go ahead. Bleat with all you've got and know that Jesus is there.

> He takes care of his flock like a shepherd.
> He gathers the lambs in his arms.
> He carries them close to his heart.
> — Isaiah 40:11, NIrV

Being called involves God initiating an intimate relationship with us and our responding by going to him. Many times being called involves a deliberate action on our part in which we step away from whatever is holding us back from knowing him more fully.

I have to add, though, that I have seen many situations in which a person was too broken to move from where he or she was to go to God. All that individual could do was cry out and wait. Jesus came and lifted up that person. He carried him or her close to his heart.

My friend Donna told me a great example of what it looks like to be called out and to respond. When she was in high school, she and some chatty girlfriends were standing in a closed circle at lunchtime talking about the guys across the way. One of the football players in the group of guys had his eye on Donna. They were acquainted but didn't have a close relationship.

That afternoon when he caught her eye, he gave her a nod and then a come-here gesture with a tilt of his head. She wasn't about to leave the safety of her group of friends and walk over to the group of guys. What if his subtle message hadn't been intended for her? What if she went up to him and he ignored her? What would her girlfriends say? None of them seemed to have noticed the silent message.

Donna shot him another look. She tried to appear open. Hopeful. Willing.

He read her expression and did a daring thing. He left the cool group of fellow football players and strode across the school courtyard. Going right up to Donna, he reached for her hand and drew her out of the group. He made that deliberate move because he wanted to have a relationship with her. He called her out of the group and drew her to himself.

The daring move worked. They've been married for more than thirty years.

In the same way, Jesus has called us out.

Whether you realize it or not, God is calling you out daily. Every moment of every day. He is waiting. He is there. He wants you. He does not give up. He longs for you to catch his gaze, read his invitation, and come to him. He will go to any length to win your heart. And here's the crazy thing — he did.

He formed you and created you in his image.

But there you were, the girl who wanted to take control of her life and be her own god, thinking she knew better than he did. You were the one who went your own way. Because of sin, God couldn't be in relationship with you, because he is perfectly holy and righteous and can't look on sin. You got what you wanted, but it turned out not to be what you wanted after all. You ended up in a dungeon far away from him. You were the damsel in distress.

That's why God sent his Son to rescue you.

When Jesus died on the cross, he called out to you — you might say he proposed to you — saying, "I love you. I want to be with you forever. I'm taking your judgment, your sin, your shame and guilt, the wrath that you deserve to die for, and I am taking it upon myself. I'm exchanging your clothes of wickedness for my robe of righteousness. Here, you are clothed with a royal gown. I want you. Won't you be mine?"

On the third day Christ rose from the grave, showing that God had accepted his payment for your sin. It is finished. Your sin is no more. Your shame is no more. Your guilt is no more.

Now God is holding his arms wide open to you. He is calling out to you. He is longing for you. He wants to be with you. He wants you to be his beloved — all of you. Your heart, your mind, your soul, your hopes, your dreams, your pains, your fears, your struggles — he wants you.

Will you say yes? The choice is up to you.

But you are a chosen people, a royal priesthood, a holy nation, God's special possession, that you may declare the praises of him who called you out of darkness into his wonderful light.
— 1 Peter 2:9

WHAT DO YOU THINK?

1. What or who is keeping you from being in a fully committed relationship with the Lord?

2. In what ways do you think God might be calling you out of darkness? Think about the friends you have, the sort of entertainment you engage in, your secret thoughts and actions.

3. Recall a time of loss, hurt, or rejection that cut deep into your life. What or who helped you to heal and to be restored?

4. How does it feel when you think about being chosen and called out from the darkness?

5. Is any shame, guilt, or sin weighing you down or preventing you from fully running into the Lord's arms? Read Psalm 103:12; Micah 7:19; and 1 John 1:9. What do those verses say about your sin?

■ ■ ■ ■

SIX:
YOU ARE OF
GREAT VALUE

■ ■ ■ ■

You might have observed by now that the concept that you are *spoken for* sometimes takes awhile to journey from your thoughts all the way to your heart. Embracing who you are and whose you are might include a bit of work, but this is good work. It's the work of letting go, leaving the lies behind, and leaning in closer to the Savior until you can hear his heart beating for you.

Here's a review of what we've looked at so far:

• You are wanted by God.
• You are pursued by God.
• You are deeply loved by God.
• You have been called by God.

And, now, the next truth: you are of great value to God.

The wonderful thing about belonging to Christ is that first and foremost he wants us to *be* with him. He highly values our relationship in the same way we prize our relationships with our closest friends and family, only more so. True friends love being with each other even when they're not doing anything. They don't have to *do*. They can just *be*. They can hang out, sit together on the porch swing, and talk about anything and everything. True friends make each other laugh and comfort each other when hard times come.

Think about how different the interaction is in a relationship between a master and a servant. A servant must continually work to keep the relationship going with the master. Servants have assigned tasks and expectations, and they are compelled to *do;* they aren't free to simply *be*.

A servant would never follow the master into the bedroom, stretch out on the bed slumber-party style, and say, "So, let me tell you what happened. This day has been insane!"

Jesus described the difference in relationships to his disciples in John 15:15. He told them that he no longer called them servants because a servant doesn't know what the master is doing. Instead, he told them they were his friends. He welcomed them into a close, everyday, intimate friendship with him. That is the kind of relationship he wants to have with us.

I am the vine; you are the branches. If you remain in me and I in you, you will bear much fruit; apart from me you can do nothing.
— John 15:5

So many people don't enter into that level of sweet, deep friendship with the Lord because they go through their lives with a master-servant mentality toward Christ. They believe the lie that it's up to them to *do* something important and valuable for God.

The truth is we aren't of any great use to God.

Did you catch that? We aren't of any great use to God. He can do whatever he wants; he doesn't need us to be puppets, servants, or envoys to *do* his work for him. The only way anything happens for his kingdom is when he gives us the power and invites us to come alongside him and to be part of what he is already doing. God *can* use us, and he does all the time. But in and of ourselves we aren't of any great use to God.

However, we are of great value to him.

Being of great value is different from being of great use.

You are precious to me.
You are honored, and I love you.

— Isaiah 43:4, NLT

Robin

I remember where I was sitting as I was typing the last few chapters of *Love Finds You in Sunset Beach, Hawaii.* The novel is about Sierra Jensen, a character who was friends with Christy in the Christy Miller Series and is the main character in the Sierra Jensen Series.

In the *Love Finds You* novel, Sierra has spent the last five years serving, serving, serving in Brazil. She is a missionary woman, and she would never trade the five years of hard work. However, her position has been phased out, and she is burned out.

I was writing a scene in which Sierra is in the car with Mariana, her friend from Brazil. They are on vacation on the island of Oahu, and Mariana is trying to help Sierra make sense of what her life had been about and what she is going to do next.

The scene is memorable even though I wrote the book a number of years ago. As I sat at the kitchen table typing, I glanced out the window at the swaying palm tree and asked myself the same questions Sierra was asking. My husband and I had just moved to Maui, and I was trying to find my place. I was used to serving alongside my husband in youth ministry and a variety of other ministries over the years. But with the move our lives had changed dramatically. I was praying about what to write next, which speaking events to commit to, and how to be involved in the local ministry at our church.

I felt as if I had given my problem to Sierra and then sat back and kept writing, hoping she would somehow solve the dilemma for both of us.

Sometimes when I'm writing I don't think about the words ahead of time. Dozens of possibilities of what might happen in the story blip through my thoughts like happy fireflies on a summer night in Tennessee. They blink, they flit, they do loop-de-loops, and I chase them all over the place, barefoot and giggling until I catch one. On rare occasions it's as if the firefly perches on my fingertip and rests there contentedly. That's when I know I don't need to scurry after any of the other thoughts. This is the one. I did not go after it. It came to me.

That's how it was with the answer to the dilemma that I shared with Sierra. The truth spilled out of Mariana's mouth:

"I have looked for love for a long time in a lot of places. I know many times over what love is not. And I also know what love is when I see it. You love God. I know that. Now, I think you will be able to love him even better if you can stop trying to make God proud of you."

Sierra felt as if the world had stopped. All was silent. The only sound she heard was the whispered echo of Mariana's last sentence: Stop trying to make God proud of you.

I stopped typing, sat back, and knew that I had fallen into a mind-set of believing I was serving God best with all the things I could *do* for him. Right along with Sierra, at that moment I realigned my heart to simply *be* with him, and the pressure I'd been feeling lifted. Instead of leaping ahead of the Lord with all my clever plans, I fell back in step with him, with his timing, with his way of doing things.

That's when I saw that I was of no great use to God, especially when I was busy, busy doing things to make him proud of me. I could see that, instead, I was of great value to him, especially when I was living with him as the vine and me as the branch. Every bit of life-giving hope, joy, and direction flowed from him. All I had to do was *be* connected to him.

> Remain joined to me, and I will remain joined to you. No branch can bear fruit by itself. It must remain joined to the vine. In the same way, you can't bear fruit unless you remain joined to me.
> — John 15:4, NIrV

Have you ever watched one of those television programs in which people learn that something they own has great value? I heard about one of those shows in which a man was asking for an appraisal of an old oil painting. I think the painting was of a vase of flowers. It was pretty. Not amazing. Not the sort of painting that would make you stop and stare as you admired the details. The frame was old and not in very good shape. As the appraiser took a closer look, his eyes grew wide.

"What is it?" the owner of the painting asked. "What do you see?" For years the owner had seen nothing special about the painting. He just knew it was old and might qualify as an antique.

The appraiser carefully peeled back the crinkled and faded paper affixed to the backside of the painting and caught his breath. Calling several other specialists to come see what he had discovered, the appraiser paused a moment to gaze in awe. The others leaned in. There was a large document on parchment paper.

The onlookers began to murmur. "Could it be? Do you think it's one of the original copies of the Declaration of Independence?"

"If it is," the appraiser said reverently, "it's priceless."

"Priceless?" The owner was stunned. "I thought it was just an old painting."

The document was examined by a round of experts and found to be authentic. It was of great value. In fact, it was priceless.

"How did you know to look inside?" the owner asked the appraiser.

"It was the signature that gave it away. When the Revolutionary War broke out, the important documents were hidden for safekeeping. So, when I saw the name written on the bottom of the painting, I knew who he was. I knew he may have hidden this priceless treasure where no one else could find it."

I just love that story.

It's such a perfect analogy of how we carry around priceless treasure inside us. Others might look at the outside and see only what seems to be an ordinary, average person.

Nothing special. But if they look close and see God's signature on our lives, they know that something of great value is hidden on the inside.

In 2 Corinthians 4:7 our hidden value as believers is explained this way: "But we have this treasure in jars of clay to show that this all-surpassing power is from God and not from us." Clay jars were the most ordinary, everyday sort of containers at the time that Paul wrote that verse. They weren't cute like our clay garden pots that have a uniform shape and are often painted with rich colors. Clay jars were easily cracked, and when they were, those were the best ones to hold a candle to shine the light through the ir-regular slits.

God put his glorious new life inside of us, and all that light shines through the cracks. That way the credit goes to God. All the glory is his.

We can't increase our value by anything we do. We simply are. And what we are is his, with his power tucked inside us. God entrusts to us all his riches — his "love, joy, peace, patience, kindness, goodness, faith-fulness, gentleness and self-control" (Gala-tians 5:22–23, TLB).

I once told some teenage girls that it wasn't a problem if they weren't beautiful by the time they were sixteen. But it was a problem if they weren't beautiful by the time they were sixty. They looked at me with bewildered expressions.

I explained that any young woman can look ordinary and unimpressive based on her outward appearance. She can try all the makeup and makeovers and make-dos to alter the outside. But what's on the inside is what will last forever. When that young woman's true self is in Christ, she is like the painting; she is carrying a hidden treasure.

The thing about carrying that much eternal glory inside your unhindered heart is that it's going to leak through as the cracks and wrinkles start to show. By the time a woman is sixty, if she has spent her days with Christ, as his friend, he has been set free in her spirit to do a lasting sort of makeover. The heart's makeover.

Sixty is the age when true beauty shows up by way of loving touches, eye-crinkling joy, tranquil expressions, patient moments, kind words, and an overall loveliness that radiates from the inside. That kind of beauty can't be replicated by Botox or a face-lift. It's real. It's eternal. And it's of great value.

Your beauty comes from inside you. It is the beauty of a gentle and quiet spirit.

Beauty like that doesn't fade away. God places great value on it.

— 1 Peter 3:4, NIrV

Alyssa

When I was sixteen years old, a couple of years after I started to follow Jesus, I also started to follow the world's view of self-image. Somewhere along the line I forgot that I was of great value to the Lord, forgot who I was in him. Yes, I loved Jesus with all my heart, but I started to be more interested in gaining the attention of guys.

The world tells us that beautiful is skinny. That message is all around us, in movies, magazines, billboards, and television. Lose this amount of weight, be this size, "be the better you." In high school I wanted to fit in, and I wanted a boyfriend. I looked around me, and it seemed as though the skinny girls had boyfriends. So I concluded I had to be skinny to gain a guy's attention. What started out as a desire to be wanted or to have attention slowly formed into a habit that lasted six years.

All through high school and off and on throughout college, I had an eating disorder. I wanted a guy's attention, and I wanted to control my life. As women, we tend to struggle with our desire to be in control.

But the Lord never said that's okay.

In fact, his directives are the exact opposite. He commands that we give up control and that we trust in him, the only One who truly has control. His control is not harsh, but rather he maneuvers situations with wisdom, power, and abundant love. He causes events that are for our good and for his glory. All that he does is out of love for us.

For me, eating was one thing I felt I could control. When life was out of my control — studying for a test, not having a boyfriend, feeling lonely — I turned to eating, or the lack of eating, because that's something I could control. I would count every calorie and plan out what I was going to eat the next day. Slowly I began to eat less and less. Desiring to be a size 6 turned into wanting to be a size 0.

I hid this truth from everyone. I was so ashamed, so afraid of people discovering that I had a problem, even though deep down I was crying out for someone to rescue me. I felt as if I couldn't tell anyone because I was the girl who encouraged others, who listened to their struggles. I was the Bible study leader, the mentor, the resident assistant. A few people knew — my parents and a couple of my best friends —

but when they said something, I would just push it to the side. Even though I knew what I was doing was wrong, I enjoyed it. I liked pushing myself to see how little I could eat. It was one thing I could control in my life. Except it wasn't right at all, not right spiritually, emotionally, or physically.

During this time I loved the Lord deeply. I walked with him and poured out my heart to him. But I couldn't fully give up this one area. I prayed a thousand times that the Lord would forgive me and help me stop, but I kept running back to my poor eating habits whenever I felt as if my life was just a little out of control.

I remember one day when I was walking up a steep hill to reach my college dorm room. The flowers were in bloom, and the birds were singing, yet inside I felt dark and lonely. I had just come from eating lunch at the cafeteria, where I had managed to put down a salad with a little dressing and a bit of water. My usual lunch. Oh, I had seemed bright and cheery, but inside I cringed with every bite, fearful of gaining weight.

As I walked up that hill, I cried out, *Lord, I'm so tired of this. I know it hurts your heart. I know this isn't of you, and yet I keep doing it. I'm so afraid of gaining weight. I want to fit in. I want to be skinny like the beautiful girls,*

Lord. I want to be liked and wanted. I want a guy to notice me. I feel as though I'm in a dark prison, with no light, and I can't get out. This has gone on for so long, Lord. No one understands. There's no way I can tell anyone who could help me either. I'm way too ashamed, Lord. Embarrassed. Guilt ridden. God, help.

I continued like that for a few more years. In fact, my eating problems grew worse each year. Right before I left for Maui, I was visiting my best friend in California, and she asked how I was doing in this area. She walked life with me. She asked the hard questions. And she stayed with me even when there didn't seem to be any progress or healing in my eating habits. I admitted to her that it was the worst it had ever had been and that I needed help. She told me she had been praying that the Lord would provide a mentor in my life in Maui to help me heal, to help me see my value, and to help me be transformed in this area. I began to pray the same.

A month later I became close friends with the woman who would be my mentor, a woman who had struggled with the same issue in high school and who helped me see how to eat well and how I could renew my mind with what God said about me.

When I moved to Maui, I was finally willing to give up. Let go. Surrender. Forever. I wanted to be free, to live as God intended, to be set free by his grace. That came, slowly and beautifully, by digging into Scripture and seeing for the first time how God sees me.

God weaves through Scripture how precious and valuable we are to him, how we are his treasure, his beautiful one, and the one in whom he delights. He tells us from the get-go that we are made in his image, that we are fearfully and wonderfully made, and that we are his temple. His Spirit dwells in us. Our bodies are not our own, but they have been bought at a great price.

If you find yourself doubting that you are precious to God, go back to chapter 2 and review the list "What God Says About You." Draw those truths into your heart, and meditate on them often.

> God paid a high price for you, so don't be enslaved by the world.
> — 1 Corinthians 7:23, NLT

As I pondered the truths found in God's Word, they slowly displaced the lies I had believed for so long. They wiggled their way into my heart and have stayed there ever since. Truly, he has set me free. I am valuable to him. I have worth in him. I can place all my trust in him and rest in his good control.

> Do not be conformed to this world, but be transformed by the renewal of your mind, that by testing you may discern what is the will of God, what is good and acceptable and perfect.
> — Romans 12:2, ESV

When I first met Jeff and then as we started to date, I was in the thick of healing from my eating disorder. I met him when I was at my worst but didn't say anything because I was terrified. Terrified that he wouldn't like me anymore, he wouldn't understand, he wouldn't want me. As I began to heal, I realized that an important step in the process was to confess the issue, to make it known, and to bring it to light. So when I went home for Christmas, I told Jeff I struggled with an eating disorder.

Whoa! There, I said it. It was out in the open.

To my surprise Jeff was gracious and kind. He grabbed my hand and squeezed it. He thanked me for sharing, for being so honest. And he encouraged me in the healing process. After that he asked occasionally how I was doing, and he always encouraged me to eat. Jeff loves food, so it's easy to love it as well when I'm with him.

Jeff showed me that my size didn't matter to him; what he was after was my heart. He loved my personality, my character, my love for the Lord. Yes, he thought I was beautiful and was attracted to me, but not because I was a certain size.

It wasn't until we started to date our second time around that I discovered the beauty of being completely honest and vulnerable with someone, that it's okay to take risks because ultimately I'm secure in the Lord. But that was the beginning. From the start Jeff showed me that it was safe to be transparent with him, that I had great value and was precious to him. He treated me with respect, honor, and tender love. I didn't have to prove myself; I just had to be me.

In the same way, the Lord loves us because we're made in his image. Before we ever did anything, said anything, or thought anything, he loved us. He died for us while we were still sinners — at the height of our rebellion. He gave his life for us. Whenever you doubt your value or worth, look to the cross. There you will see the ultimate proof that you are his treasure. Not because of anything you have done but because of what he did.

WHAT DO YOU THINK?

1. What would it take for you to believe — really believe — that you are of great value?

2. What lies have you believed about yourself?

3. What does God's Word say about those lies?

4. Pick a favorite verse from the list of "What God Says About You" at the end of chapter 2 and memorize it. How does that verse help you believe that you are of great value to God?

5. If you're doing this study in a group, turn to the person next to you and speak a truth from God's Word to her. Affirm who she is according to what God says about her. If you're doing this study on your own, send a note or text to a friend and tell her about one of the truths from the list at the end of chapter 2 that you want to encourage her with.

■ ■ ■ ■

Seven:
You Are a
Peculiar Treasure

■ ■ ■ ■

Did you know that God has nicknames for us? In the same way that a wife might call her husband "honey" or a sibling might call his sister "Sis," God calls us names. Sweet names. Pet names. Tender names that show once again his enduring affection for us.

Here are a few of God's terms of endearment for us:

- Peculiar Treasure (Exodus 19:5, KJV)
- Chosen (John 15:16, KJV)
- Saint (Romans 8:27, NASB)
- My People (Romans 9:25, NASB)
- Beloved (Romans 9:25, NASB)
- Masterpiece (Ephesians 2:10, NLT)
- Child of God (1 John 3:1, NASB)
- Bride (Revelation 19:7, NASB)

In each of these verses, God makes it clear that we aren't like those who turned their backs on him. We turned to him, and when we did, we were set apart. His Holy Spirit began the work of sanctification in our lives, and this process is making us holy.

It's a very personal process accomplished by a very personal God who comes to us with tender mercy and kindness. He communicates with affectionate names that remind us of what our relationship means to him.

Here's how it works. God calls us, as we saw in chapter 5. When he calls us, he does so with loving names. He then teaches us what is good, right, and true. He changes our hearts and our minds so that we begin to want what he wants.

God has set us apart from the rest of the world. We now have a purpose and a way of life that are different from what's standard in our society. As believers, we live in the world, yes, but we are not of the world. See the difference? If we were of the world, we would value the same things everyone else does and go after the same things they run after. We would talk like they do and act like they do. That's how we lived before we became his. Now that we are his, we experience a new way of life and a purpose that bring such joy because God's way is far better.

What does that process of change look like in your everyday life — school, work, friends, relationship drama, family conflicts, crazy emotions, dreams, and disappointments?

While every person's journey with Christ is different, one constant applies. To fully experience the joys and blessings of a God-directed life, our response to him must always be one of obedience.

> Now if you will obey me and keep my covenant, you will be my own special treasure from among all the peoples on earth; for all the earth belongs to me.
> — Exodus 19:5, NLT

Robin

Years ago we lived in a house that had two large cherry trees in the backyard. One August afternoon I picked a basket of luscious cherries and dipped them in melted chocolate. Yum!

My nine-year-old friend Natalie came over as I was lining up the dipped cherries on waxed paper so the chocolate could cool and set just right. She plopped down at the kitchen counter, watching me with her head in her hands.

I caught her glum expression and asked if she was okay.

She crossed her arms. "All my friends went to the movies, but my parents said I couldn't go."

"Why?"

"They said it wasn't the kind of movie I should see."

"Oh."

"It's not fair. I hate being the one who is left out. My parents are just way too overprotective. That's the problem."

I thought for a moment how to best respond. I mean, how do you explain to a nine-year-old the blessing that comes from living according to God's standards and not going along with the rest of the world? How do you explain sanctification, being a peculiar treasure, being set apart?

I ended up asking her a question. "Natalie, would you like to have some of these cherries?"

"Really? Sure! I thought you were making them for somebody special."

"I was." Giving her a wink, I added, "They're for you."

She perked up.

I grabbed several cherries by the stems. "Let me put them on a plate for you." I went over to the kitchen garbage and rummaged around until I found a dirty paper plate and then pulled it out. The flimsy plate was stained with beans and hot dogs from a barbecue the night before.

Natalie looked stunned. "You're not going to use that dirty plate, are you?"

I shrugged, holding the plate in one hand and the cherries in the other, waiting.

"Don't you have any other plates you could use?" Natalie asked.

"Oh yes." I returned the paper plate to the garbage and the cherries to the wax paper. "I have other plates. They're special plates. Clean plates. Plates that I have kept set apart from all the others."

Natalie watched as I went across the room and unclasped the glass door of the antique china cabinet. I lifted out a single fine china plate. Looking at her I said, "You might think I'm way too overprotective of these plates."

A flicker of understanding crossed Natalie's face when she recognized the "way too overprotective" line she had just used in reference to her parents' decision to keep her from going to the movie.

"I'm protective because these fine china plates are very valuable," I said. "Because they are so valuable, I want to keep them clean and set apart. That way they will be kept from harm and will always be ready for me to use to serve others."

I handed her one of the plates. She held it carefully and traced the gold trim around the outside of the plate with her finger.

"It's beautiful," Natalie said.

"It is beautiful. Being set apart can be very lonely, but it can also be very beautiful."

Natalie blinked shyly as if waiting for what I was going to say next.

"Natalie, you have been set apart, just like a fine china plate. You are more valuable than you can ever imagine. And you are so beautiful. Don't you see? You weren't created to be a flimsy, stained paper plate. You are a fine china plate."

Natalie thought a moment. "I guess that's why my parents wouldn't let me go to the movie."

I nodded. "Yes. They see you as being valuable, beautiful, and worth protecting, just like a fine china plate."

"And fine china plates don't go around getting smeared with beans and hot dogs."

"Exactly."

I couldn't stop smiling as I took the plate from her and filled it with chocolate-covered cherries. I watched as she enjoyed each bite.

"How did you come up with that?" Natalie asked. "I mean, where did you learn about being a fine china plate?"

"I learned the secret of the fine china plate from the Bible."

"Really? I didn't know the Bible said

anything about special plates."

"It does. I'll show you." I went upstairs to retrieve my Bible. When I returned, Natalie had finished her treat and was at the sink washing the china plate. I handed her a dish towel, and she dried it with care.

"Do you want me to put it back in the china cabinet?" Natalie asked.

"No. I think this fine china plate has a new purpose." I reached for a permanent marker in the catchall drawer, took the plate from Natalie, and wrote on the back of it. I gave it a minute to dry and then handed it to Natalie. She turned the plate over and read aloud:

Natalie,
You are a fine china plate.
2 Timothy 2:21

She looked at me with the sweetest expression. "You're giving this plate to me?"

"Yes, it's yours."

"And is this the verse where you learned the secret of the fine china plate?"

"Yes, it is. Do you want to read it for yourself?"

Natalie reached for the Bible and turned to 2 Timothy 2:21:

If you stay away from sin
you will be like one of these dishes
made of purest gold —
the very best in the house —
so that Christ himself can use you
for his highest purposes. (TLB)

Her eyes grew wide. "You were right! It *is* in the Bible!" She looked at the verse again. "What does it mean about being used for his highest purposes?"

"Well, what is the plate doing right now?"

"Shining?"

"Yes, it's shining because it's clean. You can see its true beauty when it's clean. A little earlier, when I put the cherries on the plate, it was being used to serve you. God's highest purposes for us are to love him and to love others. When we stay clean, we are set apart, ready to do what we were created to do. We beautifully reflect his handiwork as we serve others."

Natalie looked at the plate again and then looked at me with a shining smile on her face. "It feels special to be set apart like a fine china plate."

"Yes, it does. And I hope you remember that the next time your parents make a choice for you that will help keep your heart clean." I leaned down and gave her a little kiss on the top of her head. "Because, as you know, being set apart can also be lonely sometimes."

She nodded and then wrapped her arms around me in a hug.

When Natalie left my home that afternoon, she carried the fine china plate with great care. At her request her mom hung it on Natalie's bedroom wall so that during the hard or lonely times in the years ahead, she could look at it and remember who she was and whose she was.

Just like Natalie, when you came to Christ, he set you apart, like a fine china plate. Like a china plate, you are of great value. You are beautiful. You are easily washed clean when you become soiled by sin, and when you are clean, you shine with his magnificent glory. He takes great delight in using you to serve others.

You have been set apart like a fine china plate.

Alyssa

One of my favorite terms that the Lord calls us has always been *beloved.* It might sound old-school; no one uses that word in normal conversations today except for more traditional weddings when the pastor says, "Dearly beloved, we are gathered here today . . ." But throughout Scripture that is God's name for Israelites, for Jesus, and also for us, his chosen ones.

God calls us his beloved, meaning we are to *be loved* by him, and we are, every moment of every day regardless of what we do or don't do. He loves us with an unconditional, unrelenting, die-for-you kind of love. He has set his affections on us, and we are marked by his favor. We are precious to him, dear to his heart, held close, and forever wanted.

For the longest time I wanted to get *Beloved* tattooed on my wrist (but I never did because, let's face it, needles freak me out) to remind me of who I am to Jesus. Since the time I started to truly follow him, my relationship with him has been deep, rich, satisfying, and truly a joy, but it also has been hard at times. Following Jesus doesn't mean we get to take the easy way out; rather, it usually involves going against the cultural norm, against the standards of this world, making hard decisions, and standing up for what's right and true. Following Jesus can be hard because it's abnormal from the choices society makes. Often people just don't get it. But see, when we have been saved — when we are set apart from sin and this world and set apart to Christ — we are called to live differently. We are called "holy" (Ephesians 1:4, TLB); we pursue holiness. Not to earn God's love, but because we are already dearly loved — beloved. Knowing and resting in the truth of who we are brings comfort and the strength to face trials.

> Therefore be imitators of God, as beloved children.
> — Ephesians 5:1, ESV

I saw this truth play out in my life when I was a new Christian and a high school freshman. Something was different. Even though I don't think I could define what it was at the time, I was set apart.

That became evident when I didn't like gossiping about friends behind their backs or making crude jokes at lunch. I had lived like that before, but now that I knew Jesus intimately and understood who I was in him, I didn't want to live like that. Something in me was different from my friends. I no longer had a big urge to be popular or flirt with guys to get attention. I didn't want to go to the kind of parties that classmates were rushing off to.

I saw that those things brought a false sense of happiness. But God is the real deal.

He brings ultimate joy and abundant life.

However, when I didn't participate in those things anymore, I became lonely. The loneliness forced me to cling to Jesus and to look to him to be my comfort, my portion, and my friend.

During my sophomore year in high school, the Lord opened my eyes to see how my school was the mission field that he had placed me in. Yes, I was different. Yes, I didn't fit in and was lonely, but God had placed me there to be a light. My friends needed Jesus. They needed to see that there was something so much better. I wasn't there to save them, but I was there to love them and to show them Jesus.

May I share a secret with you? When you really love Jesus, when he is everything to you and not just a "Sunday thing," you will face loneliness at times. You may be the only one not to go to that party. The only one not to date because you don't want to settle. The only one not to dress in a revealing way even when it's popular and stylish.

But God promises that you aren't alone, regardless of how you feel. Hebrews 13:5 says, "I will never leave you nor forsake you" (ESV). God is omnipresent, meaning he is always with you. He never leaves your side but in fact is always surrounding you. One

Hebrew word translated as *presence* literally means "face." God is always facing you. He sees you. His eye is on you.

You may feel left out at times, especially when you stand up for what's right or when you don't participate in what you know to be wrong. But you are never alone. God is your Father, Friend, Guide, and Shield.

> The LORD did not set his affection on you and choose you because you were more numerous than other peoples, for you were the fewest of all peoples. But it was because the LORD loved you. . . . Know therefore that the LORD your God is God; he is the faithful God, keeping his covenant of love to a thousand generations of those who love him and keep his commandments.
> — Deuteronomy 7:7–9

God is faithful to provide you with friends who love Jesus too. Even though I struggled with loneliness in high school, I eventually connected with girlfriends in youth group. I had to step away from the old friends before I could meet these new friends. I soon realized this new group was my support system. They had the same values I did. We would pray together, serve together, and

139

hang out together. And these are still some of my best friends today.

God is all about community. He himself dwells in community as the Trinity: the Father, the Son, and the Holy Spirit. We were created *out of* community *for* community. God didn't intend for us to be islands, isolated and alone. He desires the exact opposite. We are to live life together with others, and in fact, that's the only way we'll flourish.

We can't do this life alone. We need other people, especially other believers, in our lives. I love looking back and seeing God's hand in all that has happened. I can see how he placed friends and mentors in my life to help guide me, encourage me, and call me to a life set apart.

Life is hard. There's a lot of pressure to act a certain way and to do certain things. I especially struggled in the area of dating. I didn't date anyone until I dated Jeff when I was twenty-two. (God's doing, not mine!) I remember how hard it was to long for a boyfriend but not to have any guys knocking on my door. Everyone around me was dating or going to school dances.

My mom was a huge encourager. She felt my pain, she understood my longing, and she walked through it with me. She prayed for me and encouraged me to do fun things like travel through Europe all summer on a mission trip. She stayed up late with me when I would come home crying because I felt lonely or the boy I liked didn't reciprocate my feelings. She prayed for me and pointed me to Jesus.

Then when I was in college, the Lord answered my prayers again and brought a friend into my life. She asked me the hard questions and saw into my heart. She encouraged me with what God was doing in me but also dug down deep to help me see my motives, the lies I was believing, or the habits that weren't what the Lord wanted for me. She did it all with kindness, grace, and humility. She loved me so much that she called me out in love. Calling someone out takes great humility and courage. It's an act of love because it's not for your benefit but for the other person's. It's wanting what is best for the person, regardless of how it may affect you. She showed me what it looked like to be honest, transparent, and humble.

When I lived on Maui, the Lord surrounded me with girlfriends and mentors to walk out that season of life with me. I matured as I put on my big-girl shoes by experiencing dating, breakups, and living in true community.

After I broke up with Jeff and then when Surfer Jeff broke up with me, I was a mess. I cried often, easily got overwhelmed, faced fears and doubts, was angry, and was shakily walking in faith. These women walked with me. They didn't just check in with a text, but they lived life with me.

My roommate held me some nights as I cried. My mentors had me over for coffee, lunch, or dinner and asked how I was doing. They helped me to process. They listened. They came before the Lord daily on my behalf. They pointed out lies I believed and the truth that God declares.

Community is beautiful, and every one of us needs it. Without community we'll sink. And the only way to have true community is to be transparent. To share the stuff you think about at night as you go to bed. To ask the hard questions. To encourage, listen, pray for, and speak truth to.

In some seasons community may be lacking. I feel like that now in my own life. I've felt like that in the past as well. But God has always been faithful. Every time I have prayed for friends who love Jesus or for a mentor to help guide me, he has provided. He has not let me down. It has taken time, yes, but he has always been faithful. Why?

Because community is God's idea, and he wants that for you too. A place to be set apart for him yet to belong with others.

> Friendship is one of the sweetest joys of life. Many might have failed beneath the bitterness of their trial had they not found a friend.
> — Charles Spurgeon

Peculiar Treasure, Treasured Possession, My People, Beloved, Bride, Chosen, Child of God, Saint, and Masterpiece. These are not just any names. These are your names. For you. Given to you. They are you. God looks at you and sees you as his beautiful treasure, his very own, his daughter. Do you believe that? Do you see yourself as God sees you? You are treasured. You are highly esteemed. You are close to the Father's heart.

No, we don't deserve those names. We know deep down that, left to ourselves, each of us is a mess. But because God is merciful, gracious, and forgiving and because Jesus stood in our place, those names ring true about us. They are our identity. We must take these truths and live our lives out of them. Know who you are and then live according to your identity in him.

You are his.
You are beloved.
You are set apart.

WHAT DO YOU THINK?

1. Go through the list of God's tender names for you at the beginning of the chapter. Which one sticks out to you? Why?

2. When have you felt lonely because you were different from those around you? In what ways did you find God during that time?

3. How does knowing that God is present, that he sees you and faces you, affect you and help you to live set apart?

4. What changes do you need to make starting today to live truly set apart? What do you need to walk away from or let go of that's holding you back from this high calling?

5. Choose a name from the list to meditate on throughout this week and to recall when you begin to doubt your value.

■ ■ ■ ■

EIGHT: YOU ARE SET FREE

■ ■ ■ ■

Do you remember playing Freeze Tag when you were growing up? You had to stand in place while others ran around you. Remember how your best friend would sprint up to you, slap your hand, and set you free? Free to run wild with the others.

Ah, the joy of running with your hair flying in the wind, playing with the other kids. Remember how special you felt when your friend rescued you? How awesome it was not to have to stay in the same pose anymore? Sweet freedom.

Fast-forward a few years. You turn sixteen and can drive. You can go to and from places without your parents. Mom or Dad places the car keys in your hand, and you're off. You can stay out later, spend more time with your friends, and sing at the top of your lungs when you're alone in the car.

Skip ahead just a bit more, and suddenly you are eighteen and graduating from high school. You leave your nest at home and venture off. You are now officially an adult. You can choose whether to further your schooling, find a job, or travel on a whole different path. You are grown up.

All of these life experiences are stepping-stones to freedom. Although they each require more responsibility, they still are sweet.

Now, take that feeling of freedom and apply it to your life with God. The moment you believe in Jesus as your Lord and Savior and begin to follow him, he sets you free. You are set free *from* something and *to* something. Set free from sin, selfishness, wrath, eternal separation from God, mistakes, guilt, shame, and your past. And you are set free to live fully for him. To continue to put off sin and to put on Christ. To love him and the things he loves. To run free from what was holding you down and to live a life of joy, peace, and abundance in him.

The freedom lasts forever. It's not gradual like other freedoms in life often are but comes all at once.

Yet one of the greatest tragedies in a believer's life is when the believer doesn't live as if he or she is set free.

So if the Son sets you free, you will be free indeed.

— John 8:36

Alyssa

I recently spent some time studying Hosea. This small book in the Old Testament tells how God calls Hosea, a prophet, to marry a prostitute. Let that sink in. Prophet. Prostitute. Marriage. Scandalous, right!? Here is a man of God, a man who loves the Lord and seeks to make him known, a man who walks in righteousness and integrity.

God has a word for him. A mission. Hosea waits eagerly to hear God's plan. He is ready to obey whatever his Almighty King commands.

"Go, take to yourself a wife of whoredom and have children of whoredom, for the land commits great whoredom by forsaking the LORD" (Hosea 1:2, ESV).

Now, the Bible doesn't say how Hosea reacts to this mission. We can imagine the plan isn't what Hosea was expecting to hear. He may have been shocked. He may have been disappointed. Maybe he had been waiting to marry a woman who loved the Lord as he did. Hosea may have been fearful. "What will people think of me?" Imagine the rumors that would buzz around: "Did

151

you hear? Hosea is getting married — to a prostitute." "A prostitute!? What!?"

We don't know how Hosea feels, but we know what he does.

"So he went and took Gomer, the daughter of Diblaim, and she conceived and bore him a son" (Hosea 1:3, ESV). Hosea obeys the Lord. No questions asked. No matter the rumors or ruin to his reputation, Hosea trusts the Lord. He fears the Lord alone.

That sounds nice. It could make a great ending to a story. There was a prostitute, she found her Prince Charming, who loved and cherished her, and they had a son (and a daughter) and lived happily ever after.

Sounds good to me.

But it doesn't go quite like that. As you read more of Hosea 1–3, you find out that Gomer has another son, but it isn't Hosea's.

Can you imagine the shame you would feel as a husband? Your wife is pregnant again. But it's not your child. Hosea must have felt horror, realizing Gomer had been with another man.

Here's the thing. She doesn't have a one-night stand, repent, and come back to Hosea. No, she leaves him and chooses to be a prostitute again. Even after experiencing freedom and love, she goes back to her old ways. She chooses slavery. She chooses sin. She chooses other lovers over her husband.

God doesn't forget Hosea, though. The Lord speaks once more: "Go again, love a woman who is loved by another man and is an adulteress, even as the LORD loves the children of Israel, though they turn to other gods and love cakes of raisins" (Hosea 3:1, ESV).

So Hosea buys Gomer back. Imagine the scene. He walks into the town square, where he sees his wife on a platform — naked, shackled, up for grabs for any man to buy her, to use her. Hosea shoves his way through the crowd, makes his way to the front, and offers the highest bid. He buys back his bride. His wife. He buys back the woman who left him and chose other men.

Why does the Bible contain this story? Why in the world would God call Hosea to marry a prostitute? Go back to Hosea 1:2 (ESV): "For the land commits great whoredom by forsaking the LORD."

God wanted Hosea to reenact how the Lord saw his relationship with Israel. Israel was God's chosen people. His bride. He was her husband. But throughout history Israel turned her back on God and went after other gods. How many times did the people forget God? Do things their own way?

Grumble, complain, and test their faithful and good God? Israelites played the whore. They returned to prostitution even after they had found a love that none can compare to.

But each time, God went after them. He pursued them in their mess. In their shame. In their sin. He got them back.

God says in Hosea 2:14, 19–20,

Therefore, behold, I will allure her,
    and bring her into the wilderness,
    and speak tenderly to her. . . .

And I will betroth you to me forever. I will betroth you to me in righteousness and in justice, in steadfast love and in mercy. I will betroth you to me in faithfulness. And you shall know the LORD. (ESV)

If we were to take an honest look at our lives, wouldn't we see that we are just like Israel? We are wanted, pursued, loved, and cherished; yet how often do we forget God? How often do we choose other things, other lovers, over him? How often do we do things our own way, thinking we know best? How often do we pick the things of this world over him? And how often do we forget who we are and go back to the world to find our identity?

You were bought at a price; do not
become slaves of human beings.
— 1 Corinthians 7:23

It's easy for us to fall into the same trap as Israel did. We uplift and love the things of this world more than we love Jesus. Even if the things we love aren't anything wicked, the focus on them takes our eyes off our relationship with Christ. When we choose other people and things over Christ, it becomes easy to forget who we are in him.

Halfway through my second year interning, Surfer Jeff ended our relationship, and I was broken. Brokenhearted yes, but also broken over the words that were spoken to me when he ended the relationship. The words went to the depths of my heart and made their home there.

Why did I struggle so much? They were just words. They were only his feelings and thoughts. But I couldn't shake them off. My spirit was taken captive by a lie. Three lies, actually. I started to let these lies tell me who I was.

1. I was too emotional for anyone to love me.
2. I was exhausting.
3. I was not worth it.

Let's be honest — I am emotional. Not just your typical-girl emotional either, but a bit more sensitive than the average girl on the street. I cry easily, get hurt quickly, and feel fragile often. This, of course, would wear anyone out, especially a guy! And because I was too emotional and exhausting, Surfer Jeff was done. It was too much for him. *I* was too much for him.

That's what I believed. That's what I carried around and repeated to myself.

But it wasn't true. They were lies. Three lies that I clenched tightly.

Jesus said to the people who believed in him, "You are truly my disciples if you remain faithful to my teachings. And you will know the truth, and the truth will set you free."
— John 8:31–32, NLT

I finally couldn't take it any longer. I went before the Lord and threw those lies before Jesus's throne. I begged him to show me who I was. I needed to remember who he said I was. He led me to Psalm 139, a beautiful song of how precious we are to him. These words especially spoke to me: "For you formed my inward parts; you knitted me together in my mother's womb. I praise you, for I am fearfully and wonderfully made. Wonderful are your works; my soul knows it very well" (verses 13–14, ESV).

In the light of God's Word, I replaced the lies with truth. The Lord formed my body, mind, and heart. He made me with purpose and intention. He fashioned me uniquely and knows my heart, my struggles, and my emotions.

Truth: I am not too emotional for the Lord, nor am I exhausting to him. He made me as I am. He sees all of me, loves me, and receives me with arms open wide. Yes, I am sensitive, but I believe the Lord created me that way so I can have a soft heart that yearns to bear others' hurts and needs. The downside is that I can be overly sensitive when someone says something hurtful, or I can be too emotional. But the Lord is refining me, smoothing out my rough edges. He is at work in me, and he does not give up.

Truth: I am worth it to God. He died for me so he could be in relationship with me. He will go to whatever lengths are necessary to get me. In Deuteronomy 31:8 Moses promises, "[God] will not leave you or forsake you" (ESV). No matter what. Unconditional love. Committed. Secure.

Knowing the truth didn't mean the lies went away with a finger snap. I had to choose to fix my mind on the truth, not the lies. I had to purposefully think of what God said about me and prayerfully believe it. Day by day, moment by moment, thought by thought, I chose to be intentional in how I viewed myself.

Now the Lord is the Spirit, and where the Spirit of the Lord is, there is freedom.
— 2 Corinthians 3:17, ESV

A turning point for my healing came on a gorgeous Maui morning. Janet, one of Robin's best friends, was visiting, and Robin invited me to join them on an outrigger-canoe adventure. One of the nearby resorts offered an early morning paddle in a classic Hawaiian outrigger canoe under the instruction of two locals.

The night before, I had cried myself to sleep. I was still reeling from the pain after the breakup with Surfer Jeff. The vicious lies still entangled my heart.

As the sun rose over the Haleakala volcano, we three women strode onto the sandy beach. The two guides greeted us by blowing into a conch (a huge seashell) and doing a Hawaiian chant to greet the new day. We each grabbed a side of the outrigger, ran into the crashing waves, and hoisted ourselves into the canoe.

Taking a left turn, we headed over to a cove where turtles liked to play. The water was exceptionally clear that day, and I could see to the bottom of the ocean. Today was a new day. A day filled with beauty and joy, I told myself, as I chose not to think about Surfer Jeff's view of me.

Weeping may endure for a night, but joy
    cometh in the morning.
                    — Psalm 30:5, KJV

Robin slid out of the canoe and into the water, and I followed suit. An early dip in the ocean wakes up your soul. We snorkeled around, watching turtles glide through the water and tropical fish weave in and out of the coral reef. When we surfaced, one of the guides pulled up a bright-red sea urchin from the reef. It looked like a bunch of school pencils all connected into the shape of a star. He placed the spiny creature on top of my head as I treaded water. Robin and I giggled about my cute little hat, and her friend snapped a photo from the outrigger before the guide returned the urchin to the coral below us.

I floated on my back and looked up at the bright sky. The rays of sunshine sparkled all over my salty face. I knew in that moment that I was going to be okay. That God was near, that he was caring for me just as he cared for the turtles, the fish, the sea urchin, and all of his creation.

And I was full of hope. I believed that God was with me, healing me, drawing me to himself, and preparing me for something that was beyond what I could ever imagine. He was present. And he was giving me hope, setting me free.

> The steadfast love of the LORD never
>   ceases;
> his mercies never come to an end;
> they are new every morning;
> great is your faithfulness.
> "The LORD is my portion," says my soul,
> "therefore I will hope in him."
> — Lamentations 3:22–24, ESV

We jumped back into the outrigger. (Well, Robin kind of kerplunked; it's tough being graceful when getting into a canoe!) We laughed that deep kind of belly laugh that friends share. As we held our paddles in position, the guide at the back of the canoe gave the command in Hawaiian, and we worked as one, paddling our way back to shore. I knew I was surrounded, front and back, with good friends who would paddle with me through life. Today was a new day. God was going to see me through.

If you're in the same place I was, listening to lies about you rather than the truth, let God set you free by going back to the end of chapter 2 to review the list of "What God Says About You." Don't let the lies bind you. You are free in Christ.

> You are the God who buys me back.
> Every time I run to the marketplace
> And sell myself to a lie
> You show up with a fistful of truth
> And you buy me back.
> Every time.
> I belong to you, Great God.
> You bought me back at a great price.
> May I not run from you today.
> — Robin Jones Gunn

Robin

My husband, Ross, once told me I apologized way too much. "You're always saying you're sorry for things that happened in the past or for things that go wrong that aren't even your fault."

I knew he was right. I felt bound up by a sense of failure. Logically I knew I was forgiven, but my heart still felt heavy.

I told him, "When I mess up, even after I apologize, I still feel guilty."

"That's a trap of the enemy," he said.

"A trap? What do you mean?"

He reassured me that if I apologized or asked forgiveness for my mistake, then that was the end of it. In God's eyes my error, my sin, was tossed into the deepest sea. It was ridiculous for me to paddle out and fish around to pull my failures back up just so I could hold them high to say, "Look at how I messed up. I'm so sorry."

Ross reminded me that God's Word makes it clear we have a very real enemy who wants nothing more than for us to be in bondage. He is the one who accuses us. He's the one who wants us to think we have to do something to pay for our mistakes and somehow atone for our failures. If we could do that, we wouldn't need a Savior.

But we do need a Savior! We need a Savior very badly.

That's what Christ did for us when he took on all our sin and failings. His blood atoned for our sin. He set us free.

Ross asked me, "Do you believe that? Do

you believe Christ has really set you free?"

I nodded and said yes wholeheartedly. But inwardly I still felt bad. I continued to beat myself up whenever I messed up.

Then one night I was talking to my sister on the phone and asked if she ever felt the same way, even though she knew she was forgiven.

"All the time," she said. "I know that's not how the Lord wants me to think or feel, but I do. I'm not sure if it's a result of how we grew up or what, but I always feel a sense of shame. It's like a chain around my ankle."

"Me too! That's it; you just named it. Shame. I feel ashamed even when I know I've been forgiven."

We talked some more about how we wanted to know and to feel complete release. We wanted to be free. Free from the shame.

"Okay, then," I said over the phone. "Let's make an agreement. From now on, whenever we mess up, once we've made things right with God and with others, let's tell ourselves, 'Shame off you.' "

She laughed. "I like that. Shame off you, Robin."

I echoed the blessing to her. "Shame off

you, Julie. Shame off you, and grace on you."

Neither of us realized what a breakthrough that phrase would become. We were both set free in our thoughts. The enemy no longer had a foothold from which he could pull us down with an imprisoning sense of guilt and shame. We were free in Christ because he had forgiven us and broken off our shackles of guilt and shame.

For years now my sister and I have blessed each other by saying, "Shame off you. Grace on you." We say it to each other, to ourselves, and to any friend or family member who needs to be reminded that he or she has been set free.

God knows us by heart. He knows we're going to stumble. That's why he gave us the directions in 1 John 1:9 to confess our sins. We must tell him right away when we realize we've done something wrong. We agree with him and say, "That wasn't what you wanted for me, was it? I know that what I did made you sad, Father. I'm sorry. Please forgive me."

When we make that confession, he sees us as blameless. Forgiven. We are made right before him. We are set free.

> There is therefore now no condemnation
> for those who are in Christ Jesus.
> — Romans 8:1, ESV

Last fall I taught at an international conference held in Nairobi, Kenya. One of the writers who signed up for a consultation told me he was from a neighboring African nation. He was tall, very thin, and had dark eyes that seemed to go soul deep. We discussed writing disciplines, organization ideas, and deadlines before I asked the twenty-seven-year-old what he was working on.

"I'm translating the Bible into one of the dialects of my country."

I was astounded. His task was monumental. I asked him how it was going.

"I use English translations," he said. "There are many that are easy to understand, and they are all free online."

"But English isn't your first language," I observed. "How did you master English?"

"I learned it a few years ago."

"You're so fluent. I thought perhaps you learned English in school when you were young."

"No," he said. "I only went to school until I was eight."

"Eight? Wow. Why did you stop going to

school?"

He lowered his chin and looked away. "I was taken."

"Taken?"

He looked up at me as if I were playing a cruel joke. My innocent expression must have made it clear that I didn't catch the meaning of his phrase. In a solemn voice he spoke five words that sounded like a thunderclap to my heart.

"I was a child soldier."

He watched my face, his deep eyes steady and unblinking.

I held back an aching gasp and stumblingly asked, "Do you ever talk about that?"

He shook his head, and as he did, a slow light seemed to glow in his eyes. "I escaped when I was twelve."

I sat in silence, reluctantly giving way to thoughts of the gruesome injustices that had been acted out on child soldiers to strip them of their humanity. I had read those unspeakable accounts over the years, but I never imagined I would be sitting face to face with one of the lost boys.

Then, as if he knew that my thoughts were headed to a vile place filled with images of the worst sort of depraved behavior, he firmly said, "Jesus delivered me."

I drew in a quick breath. Redemption.

Freedom. New life. Yes!

Shame off. Grace on. Yes and amen.

A softness formed around his mouth as ready words rolled out of his heart and covered us both, quelling the awkwardness and pain I felt on his behalf. The words he spoke next were from God's Word.

"One thing I do, forgetting those things which are behind and reaching forward to those things which are ahead, I press toward the goal for the prize of the upward call of God in Christ Jesus."

I recognized the verses as part of Philippians, chapter 3. I had memorized those same verses years ago. But I hadn't taken them to heart the way he had. For my African writing friend, those words were words of freedom. They were his new marching orders. All the atrocities of his past were deliberately forgotten. He had a life purpose. He was reaching forward, pressing toward a noble goal. The upward call of God in Christ Jesus had become a life-giving, truth-bearing reality, and he was free from the past. Completely set free.

The same is true for each of us, regardless of our pasts. We have been set free.

You, my brothers and sisters, were called to be free.

But do not use your freedom to indulge the
flesh;
rather, serve one another humbly in love.
— Galatians 5:13

Call out to God. Leave the past behind.
Flee. Turn your back on your old life. Run
to Jesus. He will deliver you. Then live in
that freedom.

Shame off you. Grace on you.

WHAT DO YOU THINK?

1. What thoughts or behaviors has God set you free from?

2. Do you live as if you are free, or do you hold on to the past — to lies, guilt, or shame? Explain.

3. What lies do you currently believe about yourself?

4. What truths counterbalance the lies you wrote down in question 3? Let those truths sink into your heart. Choose one verse that contains a truth to memorize this week.

5. In what ways does the phrase "Shame off you; grace on you" apply to your life right now?

■ ■ ■ ■

NINE:
YOU ARE COVERED

■ ■ ■ ■

Imagine that you are at a restaurant with friends. You've finished eating, and the waiter places the check on the table. You're about to go for your wallet, but someone else reaches for the bill and says, "I've got this. You're covered."

What a nice gift that is.

Or what if you were expecting a big bill and knew you couldn't pay it? For days you've been awake at 3 a.m., trying to figure out a solution. The invoice arrives. You cringe as you look at the total, expecting to see the enormous amount you owe. To your sweet surprise, these words are written across the bill: "No charge. This has been covered."

You would be ecstatic. Someone covered a debt you couldn't. You suddenly feel lighter, happier, more blessed than you ever imagined. You did nothing to deserve such extravagant kindness, and yet you got graced. Big time. Life is once again full of possibilities, and hope overflows.

Now let's ramp up the scenario. What if the debt you owed was for your disobedience, selfishness, anger, jealousy, and every secret rebellion against God? The price required for your sin was your very life. Your blood. Jesus enters at just the right moment and says, "I've got you covered. I paid in full with my life."

Do you see what an extravagant, undeserving gift God gave to us when his only Son died? Jesus's love for us, demonstrated on the cross, covered all our sins with God's love, forgiveness, grace, mercy, and peace.

But what does that mean in our day-to-day living?

Above all, love each other deeply, because love covers over a multitude of sins.
— 1 Peter 4:8

Robin

About four years into my marriage I had a meltdown. A whole lot of hidden pain came gushing out of a deep place in my spirit. I crumbled in our home's hallway, curled up across from the open door of the bedroom that was supposed to one day be a nursery. I tried to get as small as I could and drew up my legs to my chest. With my arms wrapped around my knees, I rocked back and forth and wailed.

The front door opened. My husband was home early. I didn't expect him for at least another two hours.

"Hey, I'm home! Where are you?" Ross called out to me, but I couldn't move. I had been weeping so deeply I couldn't turn off the tears. My sobs came in a second wave of anguish.

He came around the corner and spotted me in my miserable state. "What are you doing there? What's wrong? What happened? Why are you crying?"

I had a terrible time trying to form the words to tell him how fearful I was. A long list of anxiety giants had taken me down. My patient husband sat down in the hallway next to me and urged me to talk to him. Just talk. Start with one of the things I was feeling and go from there.

I drew in a deep, wobbly breath.

We hadn't gotten pregnant after four years. He nodded but didn't say anything.

My job was in jeopardy. He knew that and had no new insights or advice for me.

We had bills we couldn't cover that month. He had been thinking about that too.

Nothing in our young married life felt

secure or hopeful.

"What else are you feeling?" he asked. "Is there something more?"

There was, but I didn't want to tell him. It was difficult to confess how all the fears had opened the way to the painful memory of how my fiancé rejected me so many years ago. The memory had come at me like a fiery dart in the midst of all my insecurities about our future. The poison in that dart was the fear that one day my husband might also decide that he no longer wanted me. He would reject me too.

I will never forget what he did as I spoke my hideous thoughts to him.

He covered me.

He wrapped his big, strong arms around me and drew me close. He whispered that he would not leave me or reject me. Then he prayed for me. He prayed that the enemy would go away and stop harassing me. He prayed that I would trust in the Lord with all my heart and lean not on my own understanding. He asked God to give me his joy and to show me his truth.

My husband's powerful expression of love lifted me out of a deep, dark place. I had chosen to let my thoughts go to a prison, locked away from the light of God's truth and love.

Once I calmed down, I felt God's peace covering me. Faith, hope, trust, and joy all came scampering back with renewed strength.

As my husband stood and offered his hand to help me stand up, I realized that none of the circumstances that had knocked me down had changed. I still wasn't pregnant. Things were still precarious where I worked. We still didn't have enough money for the bills that month.

What had changed was my trust in God.

I went from feeling the weight of all the deficits in my life and my faith to fully believing that the Lord had this covered. All of it. It was as if the Holy Spirit was saying to me, "I've got this. Be free. You just do the next thing and don't worry. Trust me. I've got you covered."

Did we eventually have a baby? Yes, two. A boy and a girl.

Did I lose my job? No. I resigned after our son was born.

Did we pay all the bills that month? Yes. Somehow. I don't remember now where the money came from, but it was there when we needed it. God's constant provision.

Did my husband leave me? No. After thirty-six years we're still busy learning how to love each other and serve God together.

Above all, has God been faithful over all the years? Yes, yes, yes!

On that major-meltdown day, I learned that God always has it covered. Everything.

He has every day of your life covered as well. Trust him with your whole heart. Don't let fear sneak in and lock you in a prison of despair.

Whoever dwells in the shelter of the Most High will rest in the shadow of the Almighty. I will say of the LORD, "He is my refuge and my fortress, my God, in whom I trust."

— Psalm 91:1–2

Alyssa

Life can be scary at times. We don't know what the future holds. We get hurt. We are let down. We give our heart to someone, and sometimes that person crushes it. Or our unfulfilled expectations and dreams are crushed. Life doesn't go as we had hoped. Our plans fail, no matter how tightly we grasp to have control. Fear can creep in. The what-if question looms heavy. Anxiety can take over.

But God . . . What a sweet phrase. *But God* is with us. But God is for us. But God is our God and takes over. He is the King, and no plan of his can be changed (Job 42:2). Everything that happens to us must pass through his hands first. He allows it to happen, in his mysterious way, for his glory and our good.

God covers us. He holds us. He protects us. He is our Shield and Strong Tower. Therefore, because of who God is, we can fully rest in him. We can step out and take risks. We can live courageously because we are in his hands.

After Surfer Jeff broke up with me, the last thing I wanted to do was date again. I didn't want to even consider dating or getting to know someone else. I was done.

But the Lord had other ways of healing my heart. Part of my healing process was bringing my Jeff back into my life to show me what true love really was. To show me what kindness, tenderness, and grace looked like.

When Jeff reconnected with me through e-mail two weeks after Surfer Jeff had called things off, I was shocked. I quickly closed my computer, not wanting to talk to Jeff — or any guy for that matter. No thank you. I'm done. Stay away. The pain was so deep; I couldn't go through it again.

When I mentioned Jeff's e-mail to a friend, she encouraged me to pray about e-mailing him back and reminded me that, if nothing else, he was my brother in Christ. As I prayed about it, the Lord gently opened my heart to Jeff. The more I prayed, the more I saw God's kindness through my Jeff. How thoughtful that he had wanted to see how I was doing after my breakup even though I had broken his heart months before.

So I replied to him. And that began frequent e-mails back and forth for months. I asked him to forgive me for how I had broken up with him and how I had treated him since. I was humbled when I thought about how I had ended our relationship, which was so much like how Surfer Jeff broke up with me, and I knew how awful that felt.

Jeff showed me nothing but grace and love. I was overwhelmed by his tenderness, by how he comforted and encouraged my heart. He kept pointing me to Jesus and praying for me.

I eventually confided in my mom and a few mentors and friends that I liked Jeff so much, even though I had ended a relationship only a few months before and was still messy and healing. But each one supported this new direction with Jeff. There were no hesitations, no doubts.

One night in July, Robin and I got together to have a heart-to-heart. She took me to one of the glamorous Maui restaurants to have chocolate fondue and coffee as the sun set. I would soon be ending my time in Maui and moving back home.

She asked about Jeff, and I disclosed all my thoughts, doubts, and feelings to her. By this time I wanted to get back together with him but was terrified. My heart melted for him, but fear of being hurt was taking over.

What if it didn't work out?

What if he didn't want to get back together with me?

What if he had moved on?

What if I opened my heart to him and he realized he didn't want it after all and ditched me?

What if, what if, what if?

Robin listened intently and then spoke words of truth. "Lyss, don't be afraid. God is for you, and you are his. Everything I've heard about Jeff leads me to believe that God is directing you to respond to Jeff's pursuit of you. So what if it's scary? You can take risks. You can take this risk because you are in God's hands. He's got you. Be open. Walk in faith. Trust God's leading. And whatever you do, don't let fear make

181

the decision for you."

As we talked further, she pointed out ways in the past year that Jeff had fought for me. She listed Jeff's actions that demonstrated he had never stopped loving me or given up on me, but instead had waited for me. This was real love. This was the love that I had waited for. Giving. Unending. Selfless. Unfaltering love.

Others in my life saw the same things in Jeff. As I sought counsel from people I respected, they agreed that this was a good thing. This was a God thing. I wasn't forcing it. I wasn't controlling it. No, this was the love story God was writing for Jeff and me. I just had to let go of my fears and step into his work.

So I did. I surrendered my fears to the Lord and trusted in his fatherly care. I knew that the Lord was my portion, that he was faithful, and that he was good. I was covered by the Lord and covered by godly mentors and friends.

I told Jeff that I wanted to date him again. But we didn't officially get back together until after I moved home and he was working at summer camp. Thus began chapter 2 for us.

A big part of taking risks with the Lord and in relationships is our willingness to be vulnerable. We have to open ourselves up. We have to entrust ourselves to the Lord and loosen our grip on controlling the situation. Instead of focusing so heavily on the situation ahead and all that could happen, we need to place our focus on Jesus and follow, one step at a time, where he leads.

Nothing in life is a sure thing. Nothing is safe, perfect, or in our control. But the Lord says not to fear. We have no reason to when we walk in the light of who he is. I love what Mr. Beaver in C. S. Lewis's novel *The Lion, the Witch and the Wardrobe* says about Aslan, the lion that represents the Lord.

" 'Safe?' said Mr. Beaver; 'don't you hear what Mrs. Beaver tells you? Who said anything about safe? 'Course he isn't safe. But he's good. He's the King, I tell you.' "

God isn't safe. Life isn't safe. We're not safe as believers. But we are covered. We are secure. We are free. We are protected. God is good, and all that happens is for our good. Not necessarily for our happiness but always for our holiness.

God's goal is to make us more like his Son, and often that involves trials and pain. But those difficulties are opportunities to rely on our Savior, to run into his arms, to nestle ourselves in his embrace, and to walk with him.

To love at all is to be vulnerable. Love anything, and your heart will certainly be wrung and possibly be broken. If you want to make sure of keeping it intact, you must give your heart to no one, not even to an animal. Wrap it carefully round with hobbies and little luxuries; avoid all entanglements; lock it up safe in the casket or coffin of your selfishness. But in that casket — safe, dark, motionless, airless — it will change. It will not be broken; it will become unbreakable, impenetrable, irredeemable.

— C. S. Lewis, *The Four Loves*

WHAT DO YOU THINK?

1. How would you live differently if you believed the debt of all your sins was covered?

2. Think about a time someone covered your debt or paid for something you owed. How did that feel?

3. What areas of your life are you holding back from the Lord? What are your what-ifs?

4. What steps can you take today to entrust these matters to the Lord?

5. On a scale of 1 to 10, how vulnerable would you say you are with the Lord? With others?

■ ■ ■ ■

TEN:
YOU ARE PROMISED

■ ■ ■ ■

See if you can relate to this.

You're clicking around online and see a link posted by a friend of your cousin's friend's roommate's sister. It's a proposal video, so of course you click on the link even though you have no idea who these people are.

The hidden camera is slightly askew in a beautiful park setting. As the camera moves to the couple, you see the man holding a guitar. The young woman sits on a bench with a dozen red roses in her lap. The man serenades her with a song that he wrote just for her. As he sings, the tears flow. She is not the only one crying.

His song finished, the young man lays down his guitar. He takes her hands in his and draws her up to stand facing him.

The young woman's smile is radiant and expectant. The young man goes down on one knee. Then with tenderness and confidence, the bridegroom-to-be offers her a small box that holds a beautiful gift — a ring.

"Will you marry me?" he asks.

"Yes! Yes! A thousand times yes!"

The video clip ends and you sigh. Perhaps you smile and watch it again.

That tender moment of promise is something we never tire of witnessing. That's because every proposal, every love story, is an echo of the Great Love Story of how Christ invites us to forever be his. He has offered the Holy Spirit as the "engagement ring" of his eternal promise.

You could almost say that the Holy Spirit "seals the deal" in our eternal relationship with Christ. Here's how it's explained in Ephesians:

You also became believers in Christ. That happened when you heard the message of truth. It was the good news about how you could be saved. When you believed, he marked you with a seal. The seal is the Holy Spirit that he promised.

The Spirit marks us as God's own. We can now be sure that someday we will receive all that God has promised. (1:13–14, NIrV)

190

When you see your relationship with Christ this way, it's beautifully romantic, isn't it? You are promised to him. His thoughts of love are continually for you. He is preparing a place for you so that when this life is over, you can be with him forever.

Until that day the Holy Spirit's presence in your life is evidence to you and everyone else that you are spoken for. You are promised. Your affection and loyalties are for your Bridegroom and his kingdom, not for this world. Not for other lovers. This is intended to be an exclusive relationship. No false gods need apply. The hunt for the true love and joy of your soul is over. Jesus made his intentions clear, and you said yes to his proposal of a true, forever-after love.

Let the plans for the wedding feast of the Lamb begin!

I found him whom my soul loves.
— Song of Solomon 3:4, ESV

Alyssa

Even though Jeff and I had some obstacles to work through while we were dating, I knew that I wanted to marry him the first night I saw him after moving back home. We met up for dinner at Red Robin. He was so handsome, with big broad shoulders and his five o'clock shadow. His smile met mine. Big bear hug. Yep, I wanted to spend the rest of my life with him.

After seven months of dating the second time, I was so eager for him to propose to me. We were reading *The Meaning of Marriage* by Timothy Keller and were in pre-engagement counseling.

As the weeks drew closer to the actual proposal, Jeff asked a lot of questions about weddings: "How many people would you want at your wedding?" "Where would you want to get married?" "What all is involved in planning a wedding?"

To say that marriage was on my mind was an understatement! I would fall asleep dreaming of spending the rest of my life with Jeff and would pray daily, surrendering the timing of it all to the One who held our hearts in his hands.

When I look back on that time, I realize that I never really thought about the ring or tried to plan much of our wedding. I just wanted Jeff. I didn't want to spend another day without him. I didn't like being at home while he traveled the world; I wanted to be with him. It hurt when he was gone.

Finally the week of the proposal came.

I had a hunch that this week might be *the* week. I got a manicure just in case. I mean, a girl's gotta have her nails done when the man she loves places a ring on her finger!

The night before Jeff proposed, we were at his friend's wedding. We took a walk after dinner, arms around each other, once again talking about weddings. Jeff commented that he thought it was genius to buy a fake diamond — they're way cheaper and way bigger! I protested, saying that I would like a real diamond, even if it was so small you needed a microscope to see it.

I cried the entire way home, thinking that he hadn't even bought a ring yet; therefore it would be *months* before we were engaged.

The next morning Jeff and I drove to a church where he was scheduled to speak to the youth group. We hurried off when he was done (unusual for Jeff) because he had planned a special picnic lunch for the two of us at a cute beach in Gig Harbor, Washington. We pulled into the park and walked hand in hand through a meadow full of spring flowers.

When we reached a dirt path with a wooden fence, I looked up and saw candles and rose petals that went all the way to the beach. On the fence were pictures Jeff and I had taken together over the past three years. Butterflies danced in my stomach.

This. Was. It.

Jeff and I looked at each photo, reminiscing over our sweet moments together. Haleakala sunrise in Maui. Hiking at Mount Rainier. Carving pumpkins. Baseball games. Shamu show at SeaWorld. Ice skating.

As we made our way to the beach, we came to a blanket spread out on the ground, rose petals strewn about, candles lined up, and more photos. Sitting down, Jeff said, "Before we start, I want to read something from my journal that I wrote before I met you." He had written a letter to his future wife, which he had added to through the years.

This man had thought of me, dreamed of me, prayed for me.

"Alyssa, you are that woman. You are the woman I want as my wife." Then he pulled out a thermos of warm water and a bowl. He washed my feet, sharing with me how he wanted that act to symbolize our marriage: how he wanted to cherish and tenderly take care of me as my husband.

Tears welled up in my eyes.

Getting down on one knee, Jeff pulled out the ring. "Alyssa Joy Fenton, I love you with every part of me. I cannot imagine my life without you — nor do I want to. You are the woman I want to walk life with, to spend the rest of my life with. Will you marry me?"

194

With tears in my eyes and a huge smile on my face, I whispered, "Yes." We laughed, and I shouted a huge yes. We were getting married! I was going to marry the man of my dreams. The man I had prayed years for.

"Did you even see the ring?" Jeff asked.

Oh right, I get a ring too! I had been so overcome with the joy of knowing I would marry Jeff that I forgot about that part. I looked down, and on my hand was a beautiful diamond shining up at me.

"Is this *real*!?" I asked, remembering his comment about fake rings.

"Of course it's real, Lyss!"

The diamond was his great-grandmother's, and it was stunning.

As we moved through the next three months, the Lord revealed truths along the way about how engagement reflects his love for and relationship with us. That he has set his affections on us is a mystery, just as falling in love is wonderful yet mysterious.

He put his Spirit in our hearts and marked us as his own. We can now be sure that he will give us everything he promised us.
— 2 Corinthians 1:22, NIrV

For Jeff and me, the engagement was a sure thing. He had waited to propose until he was sure he wanted to spend the rest of his life with me and was ready to do so. When that man makes a decision, he jumps all in, and there's no going back!

I was ready to commit my life to him. My heart was ready. My mind made up. Mentors and my parents were in support of our relationship, and I had peace from the Lord that this was best for me.

From that day forward, every day on my way home from work, I would pray for our marriage, and I would stare at my sparkling ring. (I know, not a good idea while driving!) I would think about how much Jeff loved me and how crazy in love I was with him. Those thoughts led me to reflect on the Lord's tender love.

Jesus loves me. Jesus laid down his life for me. On the cross Jesus made a way for me to be with him always. And when he ascended into heaven, he sent his Spirit to dwell in us.

I understood in a more personal way how the Holy Spirit is like an engagement ring. He is the promise that Jesus wants me and is coming back. He will come for me the way a groom comes for his bride. During the waiting time God has given us the gift of his Spirit to be with us, to assure us of his promise, to comfort us until his return.

What a gift to have a promise like that from the Lord and to wear it around my heart every single day!

> Deep in your hearts you know that every promise of the LORD your God has come true. Not a single one has failed!
> — Joshua 23:14, NLT

In Bible times, engagement was a little different from what it is today. When a man wanted to marry a woman, he went to her father to ask for her hand in marriage. He would pay a price for her, and the father and new son-in-law would make a covenant. Then the fiancé would go away to build a home (actually an apartment that was added on to his father's house). The woman never knew when her husband-to-be was coming back, but she made herself ready and waited patiently.

So it is with Jesus. He came to win our hearts. He paid a price to the Father for us, the most costly price — his life. Then he ascended on high to prepare a place for us in his Father's home. We don't know when he will return, but we know that he will. Until then, we make ourselves ready, seeking him daily, growing in our knowledge of him and love for him.

We can set our hopes on Christ, knowing he will return for us. Whenever we doubt, we can go to his Word and remember his promise to come back. He has given us his Helper to be with us until then.

Robin

I love Alyssa's engagement story. My favorite part is the string of photos that lined the way to where Jeff and Alyssa drew close and promised themselves to each other. It's such a lovely parallel to how the Lord is with us all along the way. What if we could look at all the snapshot moments of how God has expressed delight in being with us? If we had any doubts that he loves us and longs to be with us, those images would make it clear that we are his beloved.

> I am my beloved's and my beloved is mine.
> — Song of Songs 6:3

When my husband proposed to me, it was simple and straightforward. We had been talking about marriage in roundabout terms, the way many couples do in that tenuous space when they realize they want to spend the rest of their lives together.

Ross knew that I was still cautious about letting myself fall in love. I knew that he had talked with my dad and had sought his blessing in pursuing marriage with me. And, like Alyssa, I had a feeling the proposal would be coming soon.

But I didn't expect it to happen the way it did, and neither did he. We were sitting across from each other, sharing a piece of pie, when suddenly the words "Will you marry me?" popped out of his mouth.

I put down my fork and tried to read his expression. Was he serious? I hoped this wasn't a joke.

The poor guy had a look on his face that suggested he was thinking, *Oh, wait . . . Did I just say that aloud?*

He reached for my hand and quickly said, "I had plans. I really did. I called a place to see about us going up in a hot-air balloon. And I thought about renting a billboard with 'Robin, MARRY ME!' in big letters. But the hot-air balloon people never called me back, and I'm pretty sure I don't have enough money to rent a billboard."

I had to smile because it was so Ross-like. Creative ideas are always running through that brain of his, but the man has no guile and just says what he thinks all the time. I love that about him. What you see is what you get. No secrets. No hidden agendas.

With sincerity he leaned forward and held

199

my gaze with his steel-blue eyes. "Here it is," he said. "I want to spend the rest of my life with you. I know you don't need the Goodyear blimp to come by right now with my proposal in flashing letters to convince you that I mean it. I know you believe me when I say that I love you. I want to be your husband and learn how to love you the way Christ loved the church and gave himself for her. So what do you think? Do you wanna get married?"

I said yes. Simple, straightforward. An honest echo from my heart. Yes.

We shopped together for a ring later that week, and when he put it on my finger, I felt as if our engagement was official. I was promised to a man of integrity, and soon we would start our lives together as one.

Many years later, when our son proposed to his wife, the event was a carefully organized moment at the beach in Southern California, followed by a surprise party to celebrate with their friends.

Our daughter got engaged at sunset in a gazebo on a bluff overlooking the Pacific Ocean. Her fiancé had selected that location because he had asked her to be his girlfriend in a gazebo, and he knew that her dream was to get married in a gazebo. And they were.

Promises planned. Promises made. Promises kept.

For anyone who has believed a promise that was never kept, it is an even deeper joy to watch as well as to experience a promise made and a promise kept.

Hope deferred makes the heart sick, but
a dream fulfilled is a tree of life.
— Proverbs 13:12, NLT

If you were to ask ten couples how they got engaged, each of them would have a different story. If you asked ten Christians how they came to know Christ, they would have different stories as well. God treats us as individuals. He knows what makes our hearts sing. He knows our love language. Jesus orchestrates his "proposal" moment with us and knows what it takes to woo us. He desires for us to rise up and leave all other pursuers. He wants us to be his alone, knowing that one day he will return when all is ready for the wedding. He will call to us to come away and be with him forever. Until that day, we can live with unwavering confidence, knowing that we are promised to him. We are spoken for.

My beloved spoke, and said to me:
"Rise up, my love, my fair one,
And come away."
— Song of Solomon 2:10, NKJV

God's way with us is so deliberate and creative. We were made in his image, and we have within us the same desire to show love to our spouse in specific ways that are meaningful to him or her. Jeff arranged to have the photos hung and the rose petals strewn along the trail at Gig Harbor before taking Alyssa on their life-changing picnic. My husband knew that a simple and straightforward approach would work best with me. Our son knew the exact spot on the beach and just the right gift he would give his wife-to-be when he asked her to marry him. Our son-in-law knew the moment he saw the gazebo overlooking the ocean that it was the right place to propose.

Lots of different, tender moments. Each of them included an invitation delivered in the recipient's heart language, and each proposal was followed by a jubilant "Yes!"

The proof that something wonderful had taken place was evident by the ring finger of each woman. We knew we were engaged. We were off the market, so to speak. The promise was sealed. Our love for the groom was evident by our glowing faces and exuberant expressions of affection, joy, and celebration.

But for all of us, the ultimate proposal has been offered. Life eternal with the Prince of Peace, who loves us and gave himself for us. Christ has come to us with loving words that speak to us individually. And now the Bridegroom awaits your response.

May you cry out to him, "Yes! Yes! A thousand times yes!"

Get in the habit of saying, "Speak, Lord," and life will become a romance.
— Oswald Chambers,
My Utmost for His Highest

WHAT DO YOU THINK?

1. How does the truth that you are promised to God encourage your heart?

2. Write out any doubts you have that God loves you and wants to be with you forever. Then write God's truth next to each doubt.

3. Think of at least three instances in which God has shown his faithfulness to you.

4. What, if anything, is holding you back from saying yes to the Lord? Maybe you're struggling with being obedient, taking a leap of faith, or surrendering something to him. Ask the Lord to search your heart and to help you say yes.

5. The Holy Spirit is your Helper, your Comforter, and your Seal. How can you apply his three roles to your everyday life?

■ ■ ■ ■

ELEVEN:
YOU ARE
SPOKEN FOR

■ ■ ■ ■

We hope that you've come to see your relationship with God in new ways as you've read this book. The faithfulness of our Relentless Lover is evident through the entire Bible. His tender ways of wooing us are woven through our days.

Let's do a quick review. God wants you. He loves you and is continually pursuing you. He has called you out of this world because you are of great value. You are his Peculiar Treasure. You are set free. You are covered, and you are promised to him.

All these truths add up to one strong and steady conclusion:

You are spoken for.

When you came to Christ, your name was written in God's book. You're on the invitation list to join him when your life here draws to a close. What might you expect when that day comes? A glorious celebration! At long last the Wedding Feast of the Lamb written about in the last chapters of the Bible will commence.

Let us rejoice and be glad
and give him glory!
For the wedding of the Lamb has come,
and his bride has made herself ready.
— Revelation 19:7

Robin

I've always loved Isaiah 62:4: "The LORD delights in you" (NKJV). It's humbling to know what a bumbler I am and how often I've missed the mark of what God desires, and yet he still delights in me.

That gets me every time.

The Lord delights in me not because of anything I do or don't do. He delights in me because I am his.

God doesn't have to do anything. He doesn't have to love anybody. He could have given up on all of us long ago. But his feelings for us are made known when he says that he delights in us. What an extravagantly gracious Savior we have!

That thought in Isaiah is followed by this one: "As the bridegroom rejoices over the bride, so shall your God rejoice over you"

210

(verse 5, NKJV).

Once again the Lord paints a vivid picture of his passionate, romantic love for us by using the idea of a wedding. A bride, a bridegroom. He is the One who watches us come to him down the aisle of life. As we get closer to him, we will see that the look on his face is one of pure delight, joy, and radiant love.

I can't imagine how I would have felt on my wedding day if I had started down the white runner and found that my husband's back was turned toward me or that he was standing there waiting with his fist in the air and a look of ferocious anger on his face.

That wasn't what I saw. My husband was trying to hold back the tears as his eyes were fixed on me and nothing else in the church. Just me, his bride, coming to him at last.

It surprises me whenever someone tells me that their image of God is a vengeful, fierce, and angry almighty being, seated on a huge throne and throwing lightning bolts through the clouds at us.

That isn't the way God describes himself. Yes, he is a jealous God who desires our complete devotion. Yes, his Word tells us of how his anger is ignited when we rebel against him. But through it all he still loves us and woos us, continually inviting us to become his beloved. He compares himself to a bridegroom. He identifies us as the bride. He has done everything he can to communicate the depth of his love as well as the kind of relationship he longs to have with us.

This is your chance to respond with blissful abandon to his goodness. Start living like a woman who fully embraces who she is and whose she is. Begin to see yourself as a confident bride. No wavering. No doubting. Remember, the Bridegroom calls you his beloved. Let yourself be loved by him now and know that the best is yet to come.

Alyssa

The engagement season is so sweet. You and your fiancé are committed to each other, you're planning this awesome party, and you're preparing your hearts to be one. You get to see all your closest friends during the showers and week of the wedding. And best of all, you're planning your future together.

I was glowing the whole time, either from pure joy or from sweat and tears over all the decisions. You're colliding two lives together, which is a beautiful thing but sometimes a difficult thing.

As Jeff and I continued our premarital counseling, we learned more about God's intentions for marriage and our roles, and we talked about practical things like expectations, in-laws, responsibilities, communication, and conflict. I'm thankful we had an older couple who walked through those conversations with us. They had us share our hearts and listen to each other and then helped us work out differing opinions.

For instance, we filled out a worksheet on responsibilities, who will do what in the house. We talked about if we were "clean" people. Both of us were. Who will keep the house clean? We both said we would. However, our definitions of "clean" were different. Jeff's "clean" is organized. He could care less if the toilet is scrubbed and the bookshelves are dusted. He's more concerned if the house is put together: pillows symmetrical on the couch, candles burning, books aligned just right.

My "clean" is deep clean. Toilets scrubbed, sinks washed down, dishes unloaded, carpet vacuumed. If things are a bit out of order, no problem. But if the house is dirty, no way!

Two lives are becoming one. Lots of conversations, lots of discoveries about ourselves and our soon-to-be spouse. Of course, far more important conversations unfold during this season. How will he lead you and love you? How will you honor him and follow his lead? How do you communicate with each other? How do you work through conflict? *Do* you work through conflict, or do you run and hide or forget it happened? Yes, laying out expectations and defining what is "clean" are important, but the bigger issues dominate the prenuptial time.

I loved the engagement season. I loved the time spent with my mom, shopping for a wedding dress, picking out flowers, staying up until the wee hours to make name cards and to address invitation envelopes. I loved talking on the phone with my girlfriends, sharing prayer requests, and asking them marriage advice. I loved going to premarital counseling and learning more about Jeff and how to be his helper in marriage. I loved any chance I had to be with him — registering, finding a place to live, planning the honeymoon, going on dates, and dreaming of our future together.

Most of all I loved what the Lord was doing in our lives during that season.

I had to run to him, to surrender my expectations and dreams, to trust his working, to let him, not me, be at the center of it all. He loosened my grip on my life — how I love to take control — and helped me lay it at his feet. Daily I would draw near to him and lay down all the wedding details, our needs, our future, and Jeff. I would pray for our hearts to be prepared, humble, and seeking the good of the other above ourselves. God made my heart soft, moldable, and open to his working.

Jeff, the man whom I had prayed years for, the man who never gave up on me, who pursued me despite my rejecting him, who patiently drew me out, who made me laugh until my sides hurt, who showed me what true grace is, and who often ushered me into God's presence, was to be my husband. This man who had won my heart was going to enter into covenant with me. Through thick and thin we were choosing to be together, to pursue each other, to walk this life together.

I never doubted getting married to Jeff. In my head it was a done deal, and I was ready. We did, however, get into a couple of arguments during our engagement that made me wonder if I was ready to marry him.

About a month and a half before the wedding, we were looking for a place to rent. Jeff had found this awesome house: three stories, front porch, and wood floors. But it was in the center of a rough part of town.

As we were sitting at Starbucks discussing

whether to go for this house, Jeff told me that he wanted to live in the inner city and to minister there, to have our home open to our neighbors and to shelter boys who have no dads at home. I love his heart. I love his dreams and his desire to show Jesus to this world. However, I wasn't ready to live in the inner city where cops came to your door often to make sure you were all right. Not yet. Perhaps one day, but as a newlywed who grew up in the suburbs, I just wasn't ready.

We argued. Then we settled in and talked about where we wanted to live and our philosophies of ministry. I was forced to ask myself, *Am I willing to follow Jeff wherever he goes? Wherever the Lord calls him?*

After a few days of praying and thinking, I realized that, yes, I was willing to go wherever Jeff went because I knew that he followed Jesus, and that ultimately wherever Jeff went was where Jesus was calling him. I trusted Jesus. I trusted Jeff.

When we met for breakfast a few days later to decide on the house, I went willing to go where Jeff wanted but also to share that I didn't feel comfortable in that house.

Jeff concluded the same thing. He knew that wasn't the best place for us at the time.

When I compared that experience to the

promises in God's Word, I could see how none of us needs to feel anxious about where we will dwell for eternity. As his bride, we can be filled with hope about our eternal future because Jesus made it clear in John 14:2 that in his Father's home are many mansions (KJV). He said he was going to prepare a place for us. He promised that we would dwell with him. Our hearts stir in anticipation of that day!

As fun as it is to plan a wedding, it's far more important to invest in the marriage. A wedding is one day — a beautiful, special, cherish-in-your-heart-forever day, but it is only one day. Your marriage is a lifetime. The wedding is a bonus, but being made one with your husband is where it's at.

That's how it is with our time on earth, as we are made ready to be united with Christ in heaven. One day we will be with him. How sweet it is to revel in his love during this "engagement" period. How glorious it will be to dwell with him for eternity!

On the day of our wedding, I woke up in my home of twenty-five years, knowing this was the last time I would wake up as a single woman. The wedding party drove to the wedding location, a beautifully restored barn in a field of flowers. The bridesmaids and I got ready in a cute cottage. My hair was curled, the flowers were in place, and my makeup was on. I climbed into my wedding gown with my mom's and my girlfriends' help. Strapless. White tulle. Sparkling beads sprinkled over the bodice. Silver sparkly flats adorned my feet. I was ready to see my man.

The barn held a magical glow as the lights twinkled from the ceiling. The guests were seated as the *Father of the Bride* soundtrack played in the background. Candles were lit; silver vases held baby's breath all the way down the aisle. The wedding party was lined up, ready to begin. I held on to my dad's strong arm, tears already streaming down my face as I realized that this was it. I would forever be my daddy's little girl, but today was the day that my parents would hand me over to Jeff's care, to be my protector, provider, and best friend.

The barn doors swung open. Pachelbel's Canon in D played. There, ahead of me, waited my Jeff, handsome and strong. The rain began to fall softly. All our family and friends who had walked life with us stood before us, supporting our covenant. My dad walked me down the aisle, steady and sure. All I could do was look right at my Jeff, overcome with joy. My parents handed me over to him as we all hugged. Deep breath.

Here we go.

The pastor gave a beautiful message on marriage, covenant, and God's faithfulness and grace. We looked into each other's eyes the whole time, overwhelmed by God's tender love. We recited our personal vows to each other with sincerity and vulnerability. We took communion together, humbly coming before the Lord and committing our marriage to him. Jeff gently kissed my forehead before he led me back to the pastor to exchange rings.

Knowing what was next, I was so giddy I couldn't contain it. Any second now I'd be Mrs. Bethke. I squealed and jumped just a bit.

Our pastor then said, "Jeff, you may kiss your bride."

Jeff held me close and kissed me tenderly. He cherished me. I knew it. All his words of love for me over the years came through in his kiss.

"It is my great pleasure to present to you for the first time Mr. and Mrs. Bethke!"

Everyone cheered. Jeff grabbed my hand as our song played, and we danced down the aisle, laughing and smiling from ear to ear.

Some of us spend years dreaming of our wedding day, planning what we would want, pinning creative ideas and beautiful decorations on Pinterest. Others, though, may have never given their wedding a thought but most likely desire to be married one day. Or perhaps the whole wedding-marriage thing terrifies you, or maybe you are doubtful it will ever happen to *you*.

Here's the beautiful truth: it already has happened for you. Regardless of your marital status or hoped-for status, you are promised to the Bridegroom. You already are his. When you surrendered your life to Christ, you became his bride-to-be. And one day you will be with him forever.

It's as though the Lord has sent you a love letter in his Word, and he longs for you to read it and cherish it. To believe his truth of who you are, and to rejoice in the truth of knowing you are his. You belong. You are accepted. You are deeply desired.

Can you imagine what it will be like when we are called into the wedding feast with believers from throughout the ages? One day we will sit down together as brothers and sisters in Christ, with our family, and be joined to God as his beautiful, redeemed bride. We will be clothed in white. He will be wearing a robe of righteousness. The Lord, the One who is faithful and true, the One who has "King of kings and Lord of lords" tattooed on his thigh, will come back for us on a white horse. Oh, what a day that will be! What a wedding feast to end all wedding feasts!

> Then I heard what seemed to be the voice
>> of a great multitude, like the roar of
>> many waters and like the sound of
>> mighty peals of thunder, crying out,
> "Hallelujah!
> For the Lord our God
> the Almighty reigns.
> Let us rejoice and exult
> and give him the glory,
> for the marriage of the Lamb has come,
> and his Bride has made herself ready;
> it was granted her to clothe herself
> with fine linen, bright and pure" —
> for the fine linen is the righteous deeds of
>> the saints.
>
> Revelation 19:6–8, ESV

As beautiful as weddings are and as awesome as marriage is, they are only a glimpse of our relationship with Jesus. They give us a glimmer of who he is and who he says we are. We are redeemed. We are wanted. We are deeply loved. We are fought for. We are delighted in. We are pursued. We are secure. We are protected. We are held. We are his.

We are his bride, his chosen one.
We are spoken for.

But now thus says the LORD . . .
"Fear not, for I have redeemed you;
I have called you by name, you are mine.
When you pass through the waters, I will
    be with you;
and through the rivers, they shall not
    overwhelm you;
when you walk through fire you shall not be
    burned,
and the flame shall not consume you.
For I am the LORD your God,
the Holy One of Israel, your Savior. . . .
You are precious in my eyes,
and honored, and I love you."
                    — Isaiah 43:1–4, ESV

A NOTE FROM
ROBIN AND ALYSSA

We have so enjoyed sharing with you from our hearts. Our dearest hope is that you will respond to the invitation of the true Bridegroom and step into the center of his epic love story.

We welcome the chance to hear back from you. Please come visit us at www.robin gunn.com and www.alyssajoy.me, where you'll find links to connect with us via social media.

We also want to let you know about other books that are near and dear to our hearts.

- The Christy Miller Series by Robin Jones Gunn — Alyssa mentioned in chapter 2 how these stories drew her to Christ.
- *Praying for Your Future Husband* by Robin Jones Gunn and Tricia Goyer — Robin and Alyssa used this book during a weekly study. It helped Alyssa

know how to pray for her future husband before she and Jeff were reunited.

- *Jesus > Religion* by Jefferson Bethke
  — Alyssa's husband, Jeff, wrote this
  book during their engagement season.
  It's a great resource for those wanting
  to explore basic truths of Jesus.

Now to him who is able to do
immeasurably more than all we ask or
imagine, according to his power that is at
work within us, to him be glory . . . for
ever and ever! Amen.

Ephesians 3:20–21

WHAT DO YOU THINK?

1. When you hear "You are spoken for," what comes to mind?

2. Isaiah 62:4 says that God delights in you. Do you believe it? Why or why not?

3. Are you a confident bride? What does God say about you, as his bride?

4. How does knowing that God is the Bridegroom and we, as the body of believers, are his bride change your perspective or affect your daily life?

5. Is the Lord your all in all? Are you totally satisfied in him, or are you holding things above him? Ask the Lord to search your heart.

CPSIA information can be obtained
at www.ICGtesting.com
Printed in the USA
FFOW01n0324090514
5333FF